S0-BCI-771

LET ME BE THE ONE

LET ME BE THE ONE

Elisabeth Harvor

HUNTINGTON CITY-TOWNSHIP
PUBLIC LIBRARY
200 W. Market Street
Huntington, IN 46750

A Phyllis Bruce Book
HarperCollins*PublishersLtd*

LET ME BE THE ONE
Copyright © 1996 by Elisabeth Harvor.
All rights reserved. No part of this book may be used or reproduced
in any manner whatsoever without prior written permission
except in the case of brief quotations embodied in reviews.
For information address HarperCollins Publishers Ltd,
Suite 2900, Hazelton Lanes, 55 Avenue Road,
Toronto, Canada M5R 3L2.

http://www.harpercollins.com/canada

First edition

All but two of these stories appeared (often in somewhat different
form and in some cases with other titles) in the following publications:
Event, *Grain*, *The Malahat Review*, *Matrix*, and *The New Quarterly*.

"So Long Marianne" written by Leonard Cohen. Copyright © 1967, 1995
Bad Monk Publishing. Used by permission. All rights reserved.

Canadian Cataloguing in Publication Data

Harvor, Elisabeth
Let me be the one

"A Phyllis Bruce book."
ISBN 0-00-224554-X

I. Title.

PS8565.A69L48 1996   C813'.54   C96-930735-7
PR9199.3.H3615L48 1996

97 98 99 ❖ HC 10 9 8 7 6 5 4 3 2

Printed and bound in the United States

For T

CONTENTS

LOVE BEGINS WITH PITY

1

HOW WILL I KNOW YOU?

30

THERE GOES THE GROOM

48

INVISIBLE TARGET

70

A MAD MAZE MADE BY GOD

97

TWO WOMEN: THE INTERVIEWS

119

FREAKISH VINE THAT I AM

132

THROUGH THE FIELDS OF TALL GRASSES

142

ACKNOWLEDGEMENTS

I would like to thank the Canada Council, the Ontario Arts Council, and the Toronto Arts Council for their support during the years I was working on these stories. I am also indebted to my family and friends, and to Phyllis Bruce. Thanks also to Carleton University, the Ottawa Public Library, and the University of New Brunswick, all institutions whose invitations to be their Writer in Residence for four- and five-month periods between 1993 and 1995 gave me extra time to work on parts of the book.

No, mademoiselle, no, madame, life is not easy. Do not delude yourselves. Nothing is easy. But there is hope (turn to page 5), and yet more hope (turn to page 9). . . .

—Jean Rhys, *Good Morning, Midnight*

LOVE BEGINS WITH PITY

"WHY ARE YOU LAUGHING?" she asked them. She even smiled at them a little, although falsely, surely, for she was feeling damp from apprehension.

But they didn't want to say.

Or at least no one wanted to say until a boy sitting at a desk two rows from the front decided to take pity on her and tell her that Mr. Hazlitt had a whole lot of nerve, planning to call in sick for five Thursdays in a row. And then making the school board send the same supply teacher out to the school every time.

She stared at this boy. "So that's what you think I am! A supply teacher!"

And the boy (and in fact the whole class) stared back at her in a kind of assessing wonder.

"Mr. Hazlitt didn't mention at all that I'd be coming to speak with you?"

They all only gazed at her blankly.

But when a majestic fair girl raised an arm as white as Ophelia's, Jessie found herself feeling almost mesmerized by the slide down that raised arm, of the girl's bold stack of beige-seeded African wooden bracelets, offset as they were by at least seven broad amber bangles. She made a vow to herself: I'll buy myself six or seven of those when this nightmare is over.

"Excuse me, Miss," the majestic girl said to Jessie. "But if you aren't a supply teacher, then why are you here?"

"Why? To speak to you about Canadian writers," said Jessie. "And about writers in general. About writers and writing. . . ." Her throat had gone dry. Could a person choke from dry throat? She felt that she might, her throat muscles felt as if they were on the point of going into spasm. Brad Hazlitt really and truly was a saboteur then. Which should come as no great surprise. She pictured him tearing down all the flyers she had tacked up on the second-floor bulletin boards. Forget him, she ordered herself. And introduce yourself. And so she did, and then described the mandate of the arts council while she was also drawing a dozen slim books out of her briefcase. They were from the publishing house she worked for, Ecstasy Editions. She passed them down each of the six rows and then watched them as they moved hand to hand. Some of the students politely turned a token page or two, but most only glanced at the covers and then passed the books quickly on as if they were in bad taste or contagious. Or as if no book, however beautifully it was written or put together, could have anything to do with *them*. Then there was another painful wait while she watched them make their way too fast back up the aisles to her, passed over shoulders. "Great covers," said a young woman who was sitting up near the front, and Jessie smiled in agreement even though she found some of them a bit on the gaudy side.

A young man with a mournful face opened one of the unearthly blue ones. "A book," he said in a fatal comedian's voice. "Now fancy that." He smiled at the logo for Ecstasy Editions, then said to the girl sitting beside him, "I guess they must publish a lot of erotica." Then he turned his attention back to Jessie. "Are you a writer as well then? Yourself?"

She said yes. "But I also work for a publishing house. In fact the publishing house I work for is the house that put out these books you're looking at now, the one with the bizarre name and logo. And so I put together this program on fiction writers. Because I work with writers too. As an editor. And what I'll be doing over the course of the next five weeks is talking about image and metaphor in fiction, and also speaking from the perspective of a poet—"

He peered at her, over the tops of his glasses. "You're a poetess, then?"

"Yes, a poet."

But it was dangerous to talk only to him, the others would resent it. And then it occurred to her: she should ask them who they were reading for English class.

"*Lord of the Flies* and *The Catcher in the Rye*," said the comedian. "Being just the statutory British and American books every good little Canadian schoolboy is ordered to read."

And did they enjoy them?

Enjoy—it was not a word they approved of. They made winced little prune-faces of happy displeasure and some of them even called out single words to her, to tell her what they thought of the books. "Cool," she heard someone softly call, and someone else called out "Awesome!" But then some of the others down at the back began to talk among themselves, not even bothering to lower their voices. Emboldened, a girl who was wearing rose-coloured glasses pushed at a boy sitting on the seat next to hers and it was at this same moment that Jessie caught a glimpse, at the far end of the room, of the heart-stopping flash of a note being passed.

She had totally lost control of them then. She was stimulating something too libidinous in them, she would have to make an effort to be more stern and formal. And so she aimed her voice higher to begin her little spiel. "I'd like to begin this first talk by speaking of the startling and exciting"—but the moment she'd used these two words she had cause to regret them, knew they'd be heard as middle-aged words, words of the sort teachers would use to disguise something boring, but she had no choice, she had to plough onward—"explosion we've had in this country lately, of work by women writers. . . ." And by now she was truly in a secret fury with herself because she was getting it all backwards, she hadn't wanted to begin with recent writers at all, or with women writers either—they weren't to come until halfway through the lecture in Week Three. She'd actually planned to begin with the post-World War Two writers, she had planned to read to them from *Growing Pains* and *Klee Wyck*. Which meant that now she was going to have to go backwards and there'd be total confusion.

But things were still more or less okay because a boy who seemed very pleased with himself was even raising a serious arm. "Miss?"

And Jessie felt a kind of joy. That she had survived Hazlitt's contemptuous treatment of her. That she was even being asked questions! She pointed a teacherly finger at the boy who had spoken, gave him permission to speak.

The boy smiled back at her as he got to his feet. "If you're going to be talking about women writers, do I have to stay?"

Several people laughed, and Jessie, telling herself it was important not to panic—and also telling herself that it was above all important not to act like a teacher or a supply teacher—said, "Of course you don't have to stay, but don't you want to know at least a little bit about Canadian women writers?"

"No," the boy said. And he gathered his books and pens together and then shoved them, along with his notebooks, into a zippered black briefcase, then stood to pick up his windbreaker and carry it swinging from the back of his right shoulder, on the hook of his thumb. At the doorway he turned to smile back at her with a kind of rakish pallor, and as he did so, three other boys, gathering their belongings swiftly together, also stood. At this same moment, as if they had been in training for it, the rest of the boys rose in unison, picked up their books, filed out of the room. Even the comedian was now abandoning her, although he did turn at the door to give her a terrible smile.

Jessie's heart went into free fall. She was feeling damp again, and frightened. At the same time she knew she had to think, and think clearly, and then all at once she knew exactly what she should have done to prevent this. And what she should not have done. She should not have fed the first boy his line the way a straight man feeds a line to a comic. She should instead have said, in a voice like a leprechaun's: "You may leave this room on one condition, and on one condition only. First you must tell me the names of three Canadian women writers." *That* would have kept them all stuck in their seats. No, she should have made it more difficult than that. On principle. Should have said, "And you must also tell me the title of one book by each writer."

But now she had to think of how to keep the girls from feeling ashamed of themselves for staying behind. And ashamed of themselves for wanting to hear about Canadian women writers. If they even did want to hear about Canadian women writers. But her mind was in a panicked whirl and so when the girl with the bracelets again raised her arm she turned to her in desperate gratitude.

This girl stood to speak. But the tone of her voice was immediately venomous. "I don't see why the girls should have to stay. Half this class has already been dismissed." And she picked up a tan briefcase that had a clutch of feathers and trinkets hanging from it, then turned to the girl beside her to say, "Come *on*, Deb," and Deb, who actually had a kind face and looked as if she might have allergies of some sort, shot Jessie a look that was a depressing mix of fear, uneasy doubt, contempt and pity, and then she too stood and gathered her belongings together. As these two girls began to make their way down their aisles, there was a whisperous stirring among the other girls, and at this same moment Jessie caught a glimpse of two creatures down at the back smirking in her direction while their heads were half bowed so that they could read together from the same note, and then these two grandly rose along with all of the other girls and the whole multitude began to troop past her, each nervous or brazen girl according to her own style: gleeful, spiteful, sheepish, ashamed.

Jessie could not imagine life being more of a nightmare than this: only losing her daughter Nina in a public place when Nina was a baby (which she had never done, but had always been terrified she might do) could compare with it. This can't be happening, she thought, this is the worst thing, and she saw herself slinking out of the school and even having to walk past her tormentors, and the picture was utterly unbearable to her, the most humiliating thing. And what would she ever tell the people at the arts council? And her boss at Ecstasy Editions? But at least she would now be alone and would be able to cry. Then she saw that she was wrong about this as well, she was not to be alone after all. Three people had stayed. Two girls, and a boy she hadn't noticed before, down in the back row. One of the girls had a fierce little face haloed by hazy brown hair, and the other, in jeans and a lumberjack's shirt, looked judgemental and puffy. But here they were, they had stayed, she should be grateful. And the boy, a tall, reserving-judgement, dignified young person, looked compassionate but also so carefully distant that she could imagine him praying in some locked part of himself that she wouldn't now do some new unwise thing and so disqualify herself for their kindness.

One thing he might fear was that she would praise them for being more just or decent than their peers, but she knew that she must not speak of the other students at all. She also knew that there was an almost opposite danger: that she would give her three loyalists the impression that they didn't really count because they were so theatrically few in number. After all, it wasn't their fault that they were more brave or more decent (or perhaps after all only more properly brought up) than the other students, and so she knew that the very last thing she must do was punish them with her praise.

"Is there some other place we could go?" she asked them. "Some more intimate room?" Her throat was still aching unbearably from the superhuman effort it was costing her not to weep. She could feel they were suffering from it too—her effort—that they were afraid to look at her with too much concern or sympathy, they were too terrified of setting her off.

The boy suggested the student council room down in the basement, and so they followed him down the swept concrete stairways. Jessie's thoughts were in a state of awful upheaval as they descended, she had so completely lost her sense of her timetable, the organized order in which she had planned to talk about things. And she had already given them the impression that she would first of all be talking about Canadian women writers when in fact she hadn't even brought along her notes on that part of the program.

They came into a cinder-block room, its tall windows wet with late winter rain, and Jessie at once began to speak about what she looked for in a story or poem, and then she began to read bits and pieces to them—not all the quotes were from Ecstasy Editions' writers either (far from it), in fact most were from other novels and stories whose parts she had underlined in her off-hours as reader. And now (miraculously) it seemed to her that the members of her little audience were anxious to show her their gratitude—their worthiness, even. She could see in their eyes that impressive questions were being hatched and weighed; there was the pleasurable tension in the air of words being rehearsed. She quoted Faulkner saying "Every great story is the story of the human heart in conflict with itself," then glanced up to intercept a look from the boy, and for a moment lost track of what she had planned to say next. But she had stuffed a pile of notes into her briefcase for just such an emergency, and to lead into them she began to speak of the weather in fiction and then to read them a series of snow vignettes: snow in France—Colette and her dogs out for a run on a snowy New Year's Eve in Paris and discovering the taste of the snow in their neighbourhood park: "like sherbet, vanilla-flavoured and a bit dusty"; snow in D. H. Lawrence (one of the women in *Women in Love* detesting the snow); a man in a snowed-in small town in Northern Ontario pulling open a washroom door to discover a woman sitting hunched on the toilet and smoking a sad cigarette; snow falling into the furrows of Canadian fields, Canadian gardens. Then she handed the other snow-excerpts around so that her audience could read them aloud. To the fierce little girl she gave snow in the American Midwest and snow in Saskatchewan; to the sleep-puffy girl she gave snow in Thunder Bay and snow in a Lake Huron town in early March. To the tall boy at the back she gave snow in Chekhov and snow in Detroit.

After the readings there was a small silence again, as if the snow from the books had blown into the room. It was the girl in the lumberjack's shirt who broke it with a question about voice. "I mean, what is it exactly?"

Jessie smiled the officially grateful smile of a teacher, but inside herself she felt panicked. Her mind! There was not a thought in it. But she made herself say, "Really, it's writing with spontaneous conviction. Or with authority, really. Authority and transparency. But it's also all the little ticks and idiosyncrasies that make D. H. Lawrence D. H. Lawrence. Or that make Jane Austen Jane Austen. . . ." She paused, thinking that there must be something else she should say, then said, "It's as individual, in its way, as a fingerprint. Not that Jane Austen is such a good example because she hardly *leaves* any fingerprints. . . ."

They were beginning to look edgy. Were these names they were going to be expected to know?

But she couldn't let it go. "Have any of you ever read *The Virgin and the Gypsy*?"

From their eyes she saw that they had not.

"Or seen the movie?"

No.

"D. H. Lawrence was the one who wrote *The Virgin and the Gypsy,* and you have to bear in mind that his style is extremely emotional and very physical. . . ." She wished she had something besides the testy quote from *Women in Love* with her, or could recite something suitably Lawrentian and emotional, but her memory failed her. All she could recall was Miriam in *Sons and Lovers* studying algebra and trying to learn it (according to Paul Morel) with her soul.

But the boy was nevertheless gazing at her with watchful warmth from his corner, down at the back.

"In fact," she told them, "it would be hard to find, in all of English literature, a writer more *un*like Austen—" But is this really true? she now wondered. Aren't they in some odd and hitherto unsuspected ways, really quite curiously alike? But she could hardly say that now, having already so categorically stated the opposite, and so she plunged forward. "And yet parachuted right into the middle of the first page of *The Virgin and the Gypsy* is *this* line: 'The Lord had tempered the wind of misfortune with a rectorate in the north country.' And reading it, you think: But that's not the voice of D. H. Lawrence, that's the voice of Jane Austen. Or if you look at the work of Virginia Woolf, say, you can see how much she's been influenced by E. M. Forster, and also by a nineteenth-century English writer named Edmund Gosse, even though he didn't have one-twentieth of her talent and only ever wrote one really good book. . . ."

She had lost them again. ". . . called *Father and Son*," she said.

The boy stared at her.

She didn't know what to do next. A favourite line from *The Virgin and the Gypsy* came to her: "The children began to play again, like little wild animals, quiet and busy," but she didn't think it was the right moment to quote that. And so she only said, "Did any of you see the movie of *Women in Love*?"

No.

But then the boy put up his hand. "I've read *Lady Chatterley's*

Lover," he said, and Jessie (grateful to him) and the girls (grateful to him too) all laughed.

He waited for her after the other two had gone off. "Are you walking out to the bus?"

She hurriedly gathered up her books, her jacket, her disorderly notes. Garrison Mierbachtol, his name was. She must have it on the class list the secretary had handed to her on her hurried way in.

As they walked along the lower hallway, Garrison spoke of William Blake, John Donne, Matthew Arnold. "The big three," he said, "at least for me." And he quoted a line from Donne to her ("For God's sake hold your tongue and let me love") and a line from Matthew Arnold ("And we are here as on a darkling plain") and then he turned to her and warmly said, "A guy who's a friend of mine told me there's a parody of 'Dover Beach' called 'Dover Bitch.' Probably he read it in the *National Lampoon* or somewhere, or maybe it was some obscure poet over in Britain who wrote it, but what I figure about something that's really good, that's"—and here he bounced his right palm up and down in the air a little, to weigh the possibilities of words he might use—"really heartfelt, is that it's the easiest thing in the world to make fun of it. . . . Something that's emotional is usually a whole lot easier to make fun of than something that's just sort of toned down and ordinary. . . ."

"Risks of feeling," said Jessie. And then she said, "Someone— I don't know who—even once gave this advice to writers: 'Risk sentimentality, but just make sure you never achieve it.'"

"Wow," he said, "that's really great. I should really write that down some place."

Jessie felt a little thrill—this must be what it would be like to be a teacher. But how would you keep from falling in love with your students?

She asked him if he wanted to be a writer.

He said he used to want to. "But I don't know if I have the endurance for it. I think it would take a lot of character to do it. Like you said—to take risks of feeling."

She felt moved by him, but didn't know how to convey it without sounding glib. She also thought of something glib to say ("Believe me, Garrison honey, I meet writers every day, and some of them don't have any character at all"), but she easily repressed it.

They came down the highest of the outside main stairways that led out of the school, then passed by two girls in windbreakers who were sitting up between the stone lions, grimly talking and smoking. For an awful instant Jessie feared they might be two of the young women from her mutinous class, but they glanced down at her with only moderate curiosity, and so she passed by them unscathed.

It had been raining hard while they were in their dim classroom reading their vignettes about snow, and the real world's snow now looked shrunken, done for. It was still only early March, after all, and so too early for the winter's retreat, but it really did seem to be happening. There were already small haystack-shaped greyish white mounds of old snow bordering the damp lawns, and old winter grass was streaming like hair under shallow lakes of cold water.

They started across the football field, now coldly soggy and spongy.

"Next week we could do rain."

"So was it too much, do you think? All that snow?"

"No, no, it was interesting." He smiled down at her. And then after a small pause he said that lately he hadn't been thinking about being a writer so much, he'd been thinking more about teaching.

"Would you want to teach high school courses?"

"God, no," he said, giving her a brief shocked sideways glance that fully acknowledged the morning's earlier horror. "It would have to be younger kids. Grade Five. Or maybe Grade Six." After another moment he said, "My dad's a teacher."

She felt surprisingly disappointed to hear it; it could all too easily explain why he had decided to take her under his wing.

And then he told her that his father lived out in Vancouver. "I went out there to see him three summers ago and came down with mono. At my dad's wedding. So I just hung around out there at his place and ended up missing two and a half years of school. Because after I got over the mono I stayed really tired. Too tired to come home, my mom said." And then after his return, he said, he'd worked in a brewery for a year, before deciding to come to classes at Harlow Collegiate.

So this was why he seemed so much older than the others. She thought of telling him that her daughter Nina had also come down with mono two years ago, but then decided not to—it would be too anxious an announcement that she was a parent and so was a great deal older than he was. She said, "I *thought* you seemed a lot older than the others."

He tried to hide his pleasure, but it was there, in his eyes.

She asked him if he had any brothers or sisters. She was thinking of Nina, an only child living alone with an only parent.

"No, it's just me and my mom. She works nights though, and sleeps in the daytime, so we aren't on the same schedule. When I get home from school in the afternoon she's still asleep and by the time I get home from work at night she's gone off to the hospital—"

A nurse then. Or a doctor. "She's a nurse?"

"Yeah, she works in intensive care. And then when I get up

for school in the morning she's already asleep again." He cleared his throat to quote:

> Begin, and cease, and then again begin
> With tremulous cadence slow, and bring
> The eternal note of sadness in. . . .

Jessie felt like applauding him, he was so sweet. And when he said, "We get along pretty well though," she was afraid she might even admire him too much, that she might somehow be in danger of admiring him at the expense of Nina.

It was windy out by the bus hut, and although they stood inside the shelter the wind came in and belled out Jessie's pale cotton skirt.

"I could carry one of those bags of books for you if you want."

She thanked him, handed one of the bags over.

"This going into the schools thing—have you done it before? Or is it only our school that's part of the program?"

She told him that she had done it at one other school. "At Lisgar." Where my daughter Nina is a student, she might quite easily and naturally have added. But instead she said, "And at Lisgar it was a whole different story. The teachers there really supported the program and publicized it in advance and were totally committed to it. But when I came out to meet Mr. Hazlitt I could tell it wasn't going to be the same sort of experience out here. I mean, he just basically had no interest in the project."

"There's a lot of people at our school who seem to think Hazlitt is some kind of hero or something," said Garrison, and he did an unhappy slide of his boot over the sand left by the snow on the bus hut's concrete floor. "Which is not to say that the guy isn't a jerk." And this time he smiled directly into her eyes, a crook's smile, and she for the first time felt his sexuality, his passionate and young male cynicism.

But when the bus came he didn't seem to be planning to board it. "I have to wait for another one."

He saw her to the door of her own bus though. "So see you next week then."

She looked back at him standing in front of the bus hut, in his short navy peacoat, staring strictly ahead.

It wasn't until after the bus had turned a corner and she lost her view of him that she settled back in her seat. But when the bus briefly sped out into the open again, skirting the northern edge of the football field, she couldn't resist turning back for one last glimpse of him. Which was how she came to see that his trip out to the bus had been a compassionate invention: he was no longer waiting in front of the bus hut, but could now be seen through the side gates of the woven-wire fence, walking in a fast diagonal back to the school.

Jessie went straight back to Ecstasy Editions, but at four-thirty, on her way home from work, she stopped in at the German bakery near the Byward Market to buy a Black Forest cake. She bought flowers too, a bouquet of upright pink tulips.

When she let herself into the apartment she could hear that Nina was already home—she could hear the tinny (and tiny) cry of the music leaking out of her earphones—and as she passed by her room she looked in to see her lying on her bed with her eyes closed.

Jessie hesitated in the doorway then, trying to decide if her daughter was awake or asleep. Except for her black jeans she was a cunning and pleasing arrangement of browns: shiny brown hair drawn like a shawl across her white throat, pullover knitted from such iridescent brown twine that it seemed to glisten.

Even her bracelets were brown: braided brown leather. Or in the case of two or three of the very thin ones, braided brown and black leather. Was it possible that this thoughtful and graceful young woman was also a young woman who would have gathered up her books to walk out of a room with a visiting poet in it? Or, for that matter, would have gathered up her books to walk out of a room with a supply teacher in it? Jessie couldn't see her as one of the ones who would leave. But on the other hand she somehow couldn't quite place her among the ones who had stayed.

Nina opened her eyes and lifted off her earphones. "Mum, don't just stand and watch me like that—it's too spooky."

"Sorry," said Jessie. "I didn't want to wake you if you were asleep." She couldn't seem to do anything right on this terrible day. "How was school?"

"It was okay. But then when I got home, Dad phoned. He said to say hi to you."

"Where was he calling from?"

"From here. In town for the day."

"So how did he sound?"

"Dad-like."

They smiled at this. A smile that in both cases watchfully took the other's smile into consideration. Sometimes Nina's smile also carried a small warning about Alec: No matter how impossible Dad sometimes is, this is not the invitation to a beheading.

Jessie went over to Nina's window seat and sat perched on it, her hands tightly holding the sill. "I was at school today, too."

"Oh, right," said Nina, and she gave Jessie an odd wary look. "So how did it go?"

"Their teacher didn't even bother to tell them I was coming! And so at first they thought I was just a supply teacher!"

At this news, Nina's eyes seemed to make a cold announcement: If you were humiliated, or in any way unlucky, then I really do not care to hear about it. But at the same time she must have been wanting to hear more because she started to speak scathingly of Harlow Collegiate, said it was a dumb trendy school, said that everyone at Lisgar called it Harlot Collegiate.

Jessie felt grateful to her for her vehement loyalty. "But it would have gone a hundred times better if I hadn't had the rug pulled out from under me by that competitive little creep, Mr. Bad Hazlitt—"

"Is that really his name? Bad Hazlitt?"

"It's really Brad Hazlitt."

"So what happened exactly?"

Jessie started to tell her. Or told her part of it. But when she got to the Great Exodus her nerve failed her and she decided to doctor her story just a bit. "So then quite a few people got up and left. . . ."

"They just left, just like that? Walked out on you?" Nina's voice had turned shrill, and now she was even looking almost frightened.

"I partly brought it on myself. By letting that first boy leave—"

"Mum," said Nina. "You shouldn't call him a boy."

"What should I call him then? A jerk?"

"People in grades above Grade Ten are called men and women. At least at our school."

Jessie tried to think of the boy who'd led the mass exodus as a man, but she simply wasn't able (or willing) to do it. But then she couldn't really think of Brad Hazlitt as a man either, although he must, she figured, be at least forty-three. Only Garrison Mierbachtol seemed truly manly. "It's because I'm from the East Coast," she said. "Down there we call grown men boys."

Nina rolled her eyes. "I know. Down there when a woman calls her husband for supper she sounds like she's calling her dog. 'Here, boy! Git! Git *in* here! C'mon, boy, here!'"

Jessie told Nina she was a fine one to talk. "After all, don't you call me Mum, not Mom? Unlike this boy—correction: I mean, this man—who walked me out to my bus stop after class today. Because when he referred to his mother he pronounced Mum the American way."

But Nina had no interest in any young man who'd walked her mother out to a bus stop. "So how many people were you actually left with?"

Jessie said she didn't have time to count them. "I'm not sure exactly."

"Half the class?" Now Nina was worriedly peering at her, wanting (but also not wanting) to know the truth. "Less than half?"

"Somewhere between a half and a third, I think." How many students would half of Bad Hazlitt's Grade Twelve English be? Fifteen. And a third would be ten. Which would mean that her own little class had been made up of a third of a third-minus-one.

Jessie thought about Garrison Mierbachtol again that night, just before dropping off to sleep, and felt grateful to him all over again. The Lord had tempered the wind of misfortune with a boy in the north country. But then the memory of the two note-passing girls came back to her, along with the picture of even the comedian walking out on her, although he had taken care to cast a knowing smile in her direction—a jaunty smirk that had seemed to say, "Please don't hold my revolting behaviour against me, my dear poetess, I'm still only a young thing and so must needs do as my peers do." She had wanted to yell after him, "I've suffered too, just as you have! And I've accomplished things!" But she most particularly and painfully recalled the exodus of the girls. The ones who'd smelled of a sour animal sweat from having been at gym class, the ones who'd drenched themselves in dank and floral colognes, the ones whose breasts, beneath their shiny wine blouses or tight black jersey tops, were pointed, heartlessly pert.

And she wondered: What was the difference in age between Maurice Goudeket and Colette? She was practically certain it was seventeen years. The same number of years that could very well separate Garrison Mierbachtol from herself, if she took into consideration the fact that she'd turned twenty less than a month after Nina was born, and Nina was now five weeks away from her eighteenth birthday. And Garrison must be twenty-one by now, or close to it, having missed nearly four years of school. But then she told herself: Yes, yes, but face facts please, it's a different difference—Goudeket was thirty-five and Colette was fifty-two.

Not that most women of over fifty would have the sexual panache to pull such a liaison off. But then only Colette was Colette.

The following Monday afternoon on her way home from work, Jessie got a jolt when she caught a glimpse of one of the Grade Twelve students from Bad Hazlitt's class waiting for the bus. One of the note passers. The girl—but she had to correct herself, remembering Nina's warning, try to think "woman"—was too lightly dressed for the clear but cold early spring weather; coatless, she was wearing only a very short mauve leather skirt and a navy blue organdie blouse patterned with raised polka dots not much bigger than pinpricks. She had pulled glossy black tights on over her powerful athlete's legs, and her long black hair was glossy too, shining with cruel health in the cold sunlight. She did not seem to be aware that she was being watched, but even so, Jessie stepped back a quick pace or two, wanting to keep it that way. She might have been back in high school herself, caught at the edge of an undesired encounter and wanting not to be seen. But she also kept on keeping an eye on the young woman, occupying herself with thinking of how much she looked like a stand-in for Snow White's bad stepmother even though she was only eighteen and eating tortilla chips, not an apple. Just give her another ten years, she thought, and she'll be the Evil Queen.

And then on the following Thursday morning when she was walking along the main corridor of Harlow Collegiate's first floor, on her way to the stairway that would take her down to the student council room, she spotted Bad Hazlitt talking to two nubile Nina-like girls down by the door to Grade Twelve English. They were gazing at him as if they adored him, looked up to him, would be only too honoured to climb into bed with him. Jessie ducked into a washroom and combed her hair until she heard the end-of-period bell ring, then decided to wait even a little bit longer, to wait until the shuffling sounds of a high school on the move died away. Even though *he's* the one who should be avoiding *me,* she thought. She wiped her comb on the corduroy hip of her skirt. Duplicitous bastard. She really dreaded meeting him again although he was the one who'd behaved like a jerk. By now he would have heard of her humiliation too, and she thought with parental revulsion of the way he wore his shirt unbuttoned all the way down to his belt in what was all too clearly a sorry attempt to turn the baby teens on.

By the time she let herself out of the washroom, the hallways were deserted. She ran down the staircase to the basement and her three students.

Garrison again waited for her after class and again walked with her across the football field to her bus. Was he seeing her to her bus out of kindness or because he had a crush on her? She didn't know; either prospect made her feel younger and nervous.

This time she asked him where he worked.

"At one of the meat counters at Loblaws. The one down on Rideau Street, close to the corner of Dalhousie."

"I go in there sometimes," she said. But now she wondered if she would, or should.

"Come down and see me then," he said lightly (although she heard it as an aching lightness). "Or are you a vegetarian?"

This made them both laugh.

"Sort of," she said.

"Come and see me anyway, if you're in there. Week nights I work until nine, weekend nights it's only until six."

She said she would look for him if she came into the store. "It's not the Loblaws I regularly go to though." She felt she should say this, in case she decided not to go after all.

Watching from the bus window as he made his weekly diagonal across the football field to go back to the school, she pictured herself going into Loblaws on a Saturday night two or three weeks after her school stint had come to an end and asking Garrison to cut her a large sirloin steak. She arranged for him to say, "But I thought you were a vegetarian." And for herself to reply, "This isn't for me, it's for someone else." And then if he looked wistful, or maybe even if he didn't, she could say, "And the person it's for is *you,* if you'll come and have dinner with me tonight." But if this actually happened, and he could really come, she'd somehow have to get Nina to stay away from home for several hours. Most of the time on a Saturday night she would be out anyway, but probably on this particular Saturday night she'd have a sore throat or a fever or just plain wouldn't want to go out.

But later that evening, washing her hair in the shower, she thought of a quote that made her think twice about her plan to visit Garrison at work. A French quote: Love begins with pity. And then she could all too clearly see it. Garrison loved her (*if* he loved her) because he had seen her humiliated and so had pitied her. For a few moments this thought made her feel desolate, but then she began to find it emotional, even consoling. Wasn't pity bound to be a much more passionate word in French than it could ever be in English?

And then it was time for the arts council project to come to an end. Only one more meeting with her gang of three. Jessie got a toothache on the Wednesday night prior to her final class and while she prepared her notes and ironed a blouse, the tooth throbbed. She swallowed a sleeping pill with a quick drink of cold milk, then went to the doorway of Nina's room to ask her to wake her up in the morning.

"You're always awake anyway."

"I have a toothache, I took a pill."

Discomfort in the tooth woke her just before three. But she fell asleep again almost at once. A little after four she woke to something more than discomfort moving through the lower side of her jaw in a hot wind of pain. This time sleep eluded her and so she sat up and read for the rest of the night. She leafed through a pile of fashion magazines and then even read the descriptions of houses for sale in the weekend paper. One house had the added attraction of a shrunken living room, but after a few moments she realized that the ad really said "sunken" and she wondered if the sleeping pill was affecting her eyesight or if the distortions were only an effect of the pain. Somewhere around six she turned out her light, but the darkness was so immediately alive with optic effects that she at once snapped it on again. When she heard Nina's alarm go off at five to seven she groggily went out to the phone in the hall to leave a message for her dentist.

"Sounds like a root canal job, but at least we can start drainage," Addison told her when he called back at eight. And then he said he could fit her in for fifteen minutes or so at ten-thirty.

After Nina had taken off for Lisgar, Jessie got out the class list for her Grade Twelves. She phoned Daniella Brautman first, then dialled the number for Kim McCardle.

A man answered, his voice deep and thickly unhinged by sleep. When Jessie asked to speak to Kim, he seemed puzzled. He said, "There is no Kim here." But Jessie had the feeling he knew who Kim was. She set the phone back in its cradle. But the moment she had done it, she realized that she had dialled Garrison's number by mistake and that that had been Garrison sounding so sleepy. She dialled his number again and this time when he picked up the phone she said, "I think I just dialled your number by mistake, but you were next on my list."

"I *thought* that was you."

"It sounded like I woke you up too, so I'd like to apologize."

"No, no, I was already awake, I was just lying here, thinking. . . ." And he sounded so pleased that she even dared to imagine that he had been thinking of her.

She said, "I have a little problem this morning. I have a tooth thing. I mean, I have a pain in it. . . ." Her own nervousness embarrassed her, she thought it made her sound too young, even for him. "An ache," she said. She laughed awkwardly. "In the tooth."

"A toothache, then." (Getting to the heart of the matter.)

"Yes," she said. "And my dentist has just given me an appointment for a bit before ten. And so I'll be ten or fifteen minutes late getting out to the school."

He told her not to worry about it. His voice carefully deep, he said, "I really appreciate your calling to let me know, Jess."

It was the first time he had called her by her name.

In spite of her toothache and above all in spite of the madness of feeling the wrong kind of tenderness for a boy who was not all that much older than her own daughter, Jessie took a long time trying to decide which earrings and what scarf to wear with her new army-green raincoat. She yanked open the sticky top drawer of her bureau and tried a lemon silk, but it was wrong with her eyes and wrong with the green. Then an old silver and grey Paisley, but it looked like something someone terribly wispy would wear. Then a large square of pink. She held it up to her face. A peony silk, it was by far her favourite, but its pink was rain-mottled and the black ink of its hopscotch design had got all blurry from its having been worn too often out in the rain. But it was still what she ended up arranging in a sort of cravat at her throat, then she carefully applied a pink lipstick to match. On her way out the door she pulled an anthology of modern poetry out of her bookcase to lend to Garrison. Not just because she thought he'd like some of the poems in it, but also because she wanted to give him an excuse to see her again if he needed one.

As she climbed the stairs to the school, she looked up to see that he was standing on a pedestal up above her, smoking between the stone lions, his jacket collar turned up.

"Hi, Jess." He knelt to butt his cigarette out beside one of the massive stone paws, then braced himself with one hand to jump down to the stairway to join her.

As they came into the student council room, Daniella and Kim looked startled to see them, as if they were shocked by how right they looked together. (Unless they were shocked by how wrong they looked together.) And then after class, when Jessie was alone with Garrison once again and they were making their valedictory walk across the football field, she handed him the book. "I wondered if you'd like to borrow this."

At the dentist's she had found herself thinking of him to take her mind off the pain. And now, walking beside him, she was even more aware of the particular quality of him. She thought: He knows when to use tact and when to use bravado, he is really wise for his years, he is really amazing.

He thanked her for the book and began to politely look through it, pretending to read little bits of it here and there or at least giving out signals that he planned to really enjoy reading it. And when they got out to the bus hut he said, "How will I get this back to you when I'm done with it?"

"My phone number," she said. She dug around in her shoulder bag for her pen. "Where can I write it?"

He opened his calculus textbook to the title page. "Print it here."

While she was printing it she could feel him looking down at it.

"Which number is this? Your home number or your work number?"

"I'll give you both."

He looked down at the two numbers. "Which number is your home number?"

"The top one."

He studied it.

"The one I wrote first."

This seemed to satisfy him.

But he didn't call. Not the first weekend, not the second. It was not what she had expected; she had expected him to read the book at once and quickly decide what he wanted to say about it and then wait a circumspect day or two, or at the most four or five, then call her.

In the meantime, she thought about him all the time. She also reproached herself. She should want him for Nina. And it was true that she would certainly have liked someone like him for Nina. Someone *like* him, but not himself. Because she knew she would never be able to bear it if he came to call at the apartment asking for Nina, she was not that generous. In a novel she had read when Nina was still only a toddler, a woman had an affair with a much younger man. In London this was, during World War Two. And many years later, when he came back to see her again, she was still lovely, still carefully preserved, but over the course of the weekend he spent with her at her house out in the country, one of her newly divorced daughters also dropped by for a visit, and the daughter was lovely too and of course not yet in need of careful preservation. And so the two younger ones had fallen in love and then driven off into the future in a small foreign car, leaving the ex-mistress abandoned in their wake—felled by time and despair, those serial killers.

On a Saturday afternoon in late April, a little over three weeks after the final walk across Harlow Collegiate's long football field,

Jessie took a bus downtown to do a few errands. She travelled past Major Hill Park, all its green hills and gardens on display in the spring sunshine, but she didn't get off the bus at the top of Rideau Street, she instead decided to stay on it and pick up her shoes at the shoe repair on Bank Street. It wasn't until sometime between four and five that she found herself back on Rideau Street once again, this time in the vicinity of Loblaws, and so decided to go into Garrison's store and ask for a steak. No harm in that, I just want to see him after all, make sure he's okay. Or a leg of lamb. She walked with her coat open, her heart imploring, beating hard. Maybe he'll be free for the evening. But what makes you think he won't have made other plans, she made herself ask herself. And yet because she was now approaching the store and then was all at once in it, making her way like a shopper down to the meat counter, she couldn't really believe he'd be unavailable for the evening when she was the one who had taken the trouble to be brave. And in any case all she really wanted was to be friends with him. She couldn't really imagine having an affair with him, it would feel too incestuous, the most she could hope for would be a relationship of trust and euphoric openness—that they could be their best selves with each other. But if that was true, then why did she keep on imagining him lying on her bed with her? They were lying on her bed and they were both practically crying about their absolute impossible love.

When she got down to Meats she had to pretend to be indecisive in order to allow herself to linger. Two young men in bloodied white butcher coats were restocking the counters, then pushing their way into the big room in the back. A cold odour whiffed out of there with each hard swing and chop of the door—the smell of sawed bone and cold lamb fat and the refrigerated smell of pork chops and blood.

And Garrison was nowhere in sight.

Jessie pretended to be pricing lamb chops, chicken livers. But he still did not appear, and after a bit she wandered off to look for paper napkins and wine. Then she made her way down to the fish tanks, the fish counters. She peered in at the salmon. There was also a fish that was a perfect pink cylinder, pink as a cooked ham, but with a wet-looking reddish pink bark on it, like slippery reddish tree bark. On impulse she ordered two slices of it from the girl behind the counter—an unhealthy-looking girl with dark rings around her almost unnervingly compassionate eyes.

When she returned to Meats, an officious bald man at a nearby vegetable counter was spraying a fine mist from a green garden hose onto the collards and kale.

Jessie picked up a package of pork tenderloin slices, then set it down again, pretending to be pricing ground beef, cold cuts. Then it became awkward, her being there and not choosing anything, and so she at last said to the man watering the vegetables, "Is Garrison Mierbachtol working here today?"

"Not today!" he sang, not looking at her. "Called in sick this morning! And he's not working in this department any more in any case, he's working down at the fish counter!" And at this he raised his eyes to give her a meaningful glance. "When he's here," he said.

What was *that* supposed to mean? That he was an unreliable employee? She went back down to Fish to take another look at the Fish girl.

She was still the same, still had her young (but old) compassionate eyes, her pitted skin. Maybe Garrison was in love with her, maybe it was the right thing for him to be in love with her, they were both young after all, and the girl looked like a good girl, a girl a person might tell a life story and secrets to, and so Jessie left the store in a hurry, buying only the napkins and wine.

But on the way to the bus she thought no, he's not in love with the Fish girl. She thought: Now I'll have an excuse to phone him and say, "I heard from one of the men at the vegetable counter that you're sick. I hope you're feeling okay again."

But something kept plunging her in doom, on the bus home: a memory (and it was even a good memory) of Nina as a toddler, being lifted up high by Alec—as high as the railing of the high-rise balcony of their first apartment on a windy night close to Christmas sixteen years ago. And all of them looking down on the tiny moving lights blurred by the seethe of snow far below them on the dim network of Ottawa streets. And then as Alec was about to set her down, Nina, crankily squirming to stay aloft, spotted the big green Loblaws sign on a store far off in the Glebe and so stretched out her arms and used her frail baby voice to crow with joy, "Loblaws!"

How foolishly proud her young parents had been on that stormy night, joined in the triumphant euphoria of being parents to a child who could already read—one word, if no others— when she wasn't yet two. Alec had even laughed and said, "Listen to that, Jess. We've raised ourselves a little consumer." And Jessie had such a clear picture of Nina as she was then, her hands two plump little stars darting out to touch the distant green neon letters while the whole swarming city turned itself into a snowy cauldron beneath them.

HOW WILL I KNOW
YOU?

WHEN SHE STOOD IN THE DOORWAY to his cubicle one cold and sunny Monday morning in early spring, feeling newly shiny and slim and reading him some of the winning entries from a *Globe and Mail* contest for invented mistakes that drunken or incompetent sign-painters might make—HAZARDOUS FOOTBATH, SMALL APARTMENT FOR RUNT, HOSPITAL NOT RESPONSIBLE FOR YOUR LONGINGS—he laughed, looking with surprised alertness into her eyes, and then just before noon, on his way past her desk, he dropped a note on her letter tray while she was talking on the phone to a friend who worked in a bookstore two blocks south of the park. She kept trying to read the note while she was listening to her friend go on and on about a mad customer—mad as in deluded—and finally felt she had no choice but to interrupt her to say that someone from down

the hall had just stopped by to dump an incredibly complex-look-
ing document on her desk and she was going to have to hang up
so she could try to deal with the damn thing before lunchtime.
And feeling a little guilty but excited—no, no, no, not feeling
guilty at all *and* excited—she said a rushed goodbye to her friend
and picked up the note to at last give it her passionate attention:

Memo to Marianne,

On my way through the park this morning I spotted a hazardous footbath (it has a fountain in the middle of it, which has very sensibly decided to spout
wine, not water) and it occurred to me that we might
give it a try one of these balmy spring noontimes, and
then after we've been to the hospital for emergency
treatment for intoxication we might catch sight of a
sign saying HOSPITAL NOT RESPONSIBLE FOR
YOUR LONGINGS and at this point we might stop
to ask ourselves: If the *hospital* is not responsible for our
longings, then who *is*? Am I? Are you?

Farley

P.S. Please meet me for lunch today, twelve sharp, so
that we can discuss this matter.

She noticed that he'd erased a word before writing "intoxication" over it. The erased word was "alcoholism." It made her
feel happy that he was using the sign-makers' jokes to escalate
the already intoxicated feelings between them. It was as if the
sign-makers had, without knowing it, become matchmakers.
Personal matchmakers to two people they didn't even know and

would never know. She was also relieved that he hadn't mentioned the apartment for runt, partly because while reading the runt sign to him she had all at once heard it as "apartment for rut," but also because she had felt embarrassed for his sake since he happened to be really quite extraordinarily short.

On the way to the restaurant, though, sitting on one of those pelts of wooden beads that drivers throw over the driver's seat to ward off back pain, he looked tall. He had the chest and the powerful neck of a much bigger man. Seated, he was majestic, protectively attentive. But then she had never been one to look down on men who were short—she was tiny herself—and had often even preferred them; had in fact often found them to be braver and more scrappy than the men who towered.

At the restaurant she drank five glasses of wine to his one (but he was driving) and on the way back to the office he played her a tape of "So Long, Marianne"—she was touched that he owned it and even dared to wonder if he had bought it because of her— and then he sang along with "You're really such a pretty one, I see you've gone and changed your name again . . ." which made them both smile because she really *had* gone and changed her name, but only the spelling of it, from the prim Mary Ann to the more sexually sweet Marianne, and after they'd pushed their way through the revolving doors of their building—PLEASE USE REVOLTING DOORS, one of the *Globe* contestants had written—he said goodbye to her at the door to her office and then whispered, "So long, Marianne," in a way that really seemed to be saying "Hello, Marianne, hello, hello, hello, hello. . . ." But it really and truly was goodbye, as it turned out, because he called in sick every day the rest of the week and then the following week went on vacation with his wife and sixteen-year-old daughter, and on his return it was clear that he had spent at least part of his holiday perfecting a heartbreakingly friendly smile with no emotion at all in it. It was at this same time that insomnia moved permanently into her bed, to spend all of the hot summer nights with her. But why? When almost nothing had happened, or had had time to happen? The answer, to Marianne at least, was perfectly clear: because it took no time at all to have everything happen in the heart—ways they would touch each other, a whole life together.

But then she told herself that she didn't really want to have to go to all the trouble of arranging her life to allow another person to come into it. Why squander, she would think, her sweet evenings of solitude? And once her children were safely asleep in their beds, she would sink into a deep chair with a magazine or a novel, having already reached over to the phone to take its receiver off the hook. She would only lift it up now and then to check to see if there was a message for her on her call-answer service. The times she got a dial tone would be almost hilariously humbling—that she was going to such extreme lengths not to be reached when in fact no one in the whole world was trying to reach her.

But she continued to have trouble sleeping, and one hot day in August she walked over to the Sunshine Trading Company to buy a box of Sleepytime Tea and a tall bottle of tablets made from hops and valerian. She also picked up a copy of a local holistic newspaper called *Vital Signs*. The signs, she saw, leafing quickly through its pages while waiting in line for her turn to pay for her pills, were both astrological and medical. It also just so happened that in this particular issue a man named Ray Fennimore, the paper's resident herbalist, had devoted his entire column to sleeplessness. According to Ray, the causes and cures were complex and varied. He used a wide variety of herbs in his treatments, but had also incorporated into his medical game plan "several other modalities." *If you would like to see Ray for a private consultation,* said the italics at the bottom of his column, *call Gandee Falls 613-762-8903.*

From the phone in her office, Marianne called Gandee Falls and Ray answered. He had a fine voice, musical and thoughtful. They talked for nearly fifteen minutes, mainly about herbs for sedation. "I think I'd really have to see you, though, to sift through all the possibilities of your case."

She asked him what the charge would be.

"Sixty-five dollars per consult. But you have to bear in mind that we'd be talking on the generous side of an hour."

She asked about buses, how long it would take to get out to Gandee Falls.

"A little over an hour." And then a shorter local bus trip out into the country. About twenty minutes. "But listen, if we can settle on a date right now, I can arrange to drive in to the depot to meet you."

She thanked him for his kindness. "I could get time off work a little after two on Friday afternoon."

He said good, there was a bus in at three-forty-five. "How will I know you?"

She said she would carry a copy of *Vital Signs.*

Friday was a perfect clear day, ruffled by hopeful breezes, and Marianne, in spite of the weeks of almost no sleep, took pleasure in the trip to Gandee Falls as the bus passed through all the green and surreal country towns. Travelling by public transportation was also superbly relaxing—back in the days when she was still married to Gary they used to get into terrible fights in the car, and one Sunday morning when they were on their way to have lunch with friends who lived north of Kleinburg, Gary had flown into a rage because she had brought along a small picnic of carrot sticks and almonds wrapped up in foil. Also a banana. Which he had knocked out of her hand as she was beginning to peel it, with the consequence that when it had started rolling around down on the floor of the car she'd used an angry sandalled foot to mash it into a gritty purée and then scooped it up to paw on the front of his shirt. While he'd been craning away from her, trying to ward off the purée, the car had drifted across the median line and he'd had to fight it back to the right side again—the whole careen a desperate episode in which they had just narrowly managed to miss getting themselves killed.

There was no one waiting for her at the bus depot in Gandee Falls.

She looked at her watch. "Are we in early?" she asked the driver.

On the contrary. Five minutes late.

Had Ray Fennimore already been and gone? Marianne pulled *Vital Signs* out of her bag to glance at his picture again and saw for the first time that he looked a little unreliable and moody. His long black hair looked lankly dull and unkempt. But she told herself to keep calm. In all likelihood he would arrive any minute. She pictured him wearing a Peruvian poncho and Gandhi glasses. Gandhi glasses in Gandee Falls. The studious herbalist. She walked past a row of men sitting on a bench, taking in the scene, then made her way out to the front of the depot.

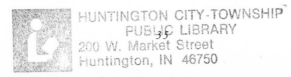
HUNTINGTON CITY-TOWNSHIP
PUBLIC LIBRARY
200 W. Market Street
Huntington, IN 46750

She stood waiting in the hot sun and tried to hold her face in an attitude of attractive repose. She could see several churches: a nearby yellow one with black trim, and three modest white ones—country churches that had somehow found their way into town—and several blocks to the left of the depot a tan clapboard cathedral dwarfed by a massive greystone real cathedral perched on a high hill of parks and organized gardens. As for the air, it was clear, almost country air, but at the same time it seemed sad— seemed to smell of ice cream and controlled sorrow. And the town's children, in their laundered pastel overalls and perfectly pressed pale little shirts, also somehow managed to give off an air of having been raised in an atmosphere of criminal neglect. The town didn't even seem to be a town in Ontario, it was too dry and church-dominated and hilly and sad, and wherever the falls of Gandee Falls were falling, they were falling nowhere nearby.

After fifteen minutes of waiting and of not daring to go inside to look for a phone in case she should miss him, Marianne found a pay phone beside the Ladies Room and phoned Fennimore's number.

But the line was busy.

She went outside again, into the hot wind, and this time she looked to the right, toward a used-car lot and back again toward the yellow church whose square steeple gave it a lonely and squat Baptist look.

Three minutes later she was back inside the depot again, back at the phone.

This time she got him.

"Oh Christ," he said. "I just totally forgot." And then he told her that he was expecting company for a sit-down dinner at six o'clock and that he'd have to somehow work in the consultation with her before the company came.

"How long do you think it'll take you to get into town?"

But he must have forgotten this part of the arrangement as well because after a startled pause he said he would come right away. "Be there in twenty minutes. Wait out at the front."

While Marianne was standing out on the sidewalk with the hot wind blowing in her hair, a car pulled in beside her. "Need a lift somewhere?"

The driver was young, with long shining black hair and dark wire-rimmed glasses, and so for a confused moment she mistook him for Fennimore, concluding that it was out of apology that the herbalist was now making a lighthearted joke. "Mr. Ray Fennimore?" she asked him, opening the door and peering in.

The man grinned up at her, uneasy but jaunty.

"Sorry," she whispered, flustered. "I was expecting someone else."

Five minutes later another car. Another stranger. A ruined anxious boy's face on a man of forty. "Want a drive, sweetheart?"

She backed up and stood against the wall of the station. She lifted the copy of *Vital Signs* in front of her breasts and held it there tightly. People would think she was trying to convert them to some old-time religion. She was by this time feeling irritably morose, and in an embittered way even relieved to be alone, as if she had been stood up on a blind date by someone she'd already decided must be bizarrely unappealing. She thought of her children, and wondered if they'd got home from school yet. She had taped a note to the door of the fridge, telling them that she'd gone to Gandee Falls for an appointment and would be home no later than seven. Now she wished that she had also given them Fennimore's name and number. In case she was late getting back. In case they needed to reach her for some reason. She could go inside the station right now and go back to the pay phone and put in a call to them. But what if Fennimore arrived while she was away from her post? She didn't want to miss him, by now all she was wanting was to get out to his place and have the consultation in a hurry, get it over and done with.

Forty-five minutes had now passed and she was beginning to wish that she'd asked him to pick her up at a restaurant, she was nearly dying of hunger, she could have been eating an early supper while she was waiting for him to decide whether or not he was going to show up.

Or he won't come at all, she thought. Never planned to. By now putting nothing past him.

At a quarter past five, a battered station wagon pulled in against the curb on the far side of the street and a big man with a grey brush cut got stiffly out. He looked straight at her. "Marianne?" he called over to her.

She crossed the street to him. She asked doubtfully, "Are you Ray Fennimore?"

"I guess I must look older than the picture in *Vital Signs*."

She was trying to hear if his voice still sounded musical and thoughtful. Not very, but she got into the car with him anyway, even though anxiety gripped her. Her mind was filled with only one thought: How could this person, at any time in his life, have been the dark young man in the photo? She saw that above his right ear he had a scar with an elongated halo of hairless skin around it. A war wound? But perhaps she only thought it was a war wound because it was shaped like a torpedo. And below his military haircut and scar, a face that suggested a well-groomed ruddy fury. She had also taken note of the fact that he'd said "*the* picture," not "*my* picture." There was also the puzzle of the car to unravel: it smelled so poisonous—of diesel oil and paint remover and spilled kerosene. Of ancient cigarette smoke too, and of old paint-spattered rags. Three lumpy sacks had been thrown onto the back seat. Beans, she thought. Or bodies! But it was no joke, the car was truly noxious, a toxic ruin. What kind of car was this for a herbalist?

But they were already driving south through Gandee Falls on their way out of the town. Very soon they would be coming to bungalows, woodlots, open country. She said in a voice that she tried to keep from sounding squeaky and small, "Do you sell food out at your herb place?"

He said no, only herbs.

She told him that she was going to be needing some food very soon, that she hadn't eaten a thing since early morning. But then a happy thought occurred to her. "Why don't we find a place to talk right here in Gandee Falls? You can talk and I'll eat, and that way we can save you the twenty minutes you'd waste driving me back into town again."

She saw by the perplexed look he threw her that he'd had no intention of driving her back into town. He said that eating in Gandee Falls was totally out of the question. "My wife and I are expecting six guests for a sit-down dinner at six o'clock and I promised to help out."

She wondered why he kept speaking, in tones of such solemn respect, of the sit-down dinner. Didn't people the whole world over sit down to eat? And at this, a mad (or possibly sane) thought occurred to her: the sit-down dinner was an invention. There was no wife, no dinner table, no casserole keeping warm on the back of the stove. There was no stove. Fennimore lived all alone in a shack out in the Ontario bush. Nothing in it but a phone and a typewriter and a few medieval bunches of dried herbs (looking like switches) and a collection of knives. She pictured the terrifying décor of the even deeper wilderness that would lie a mile or two behind his ill-equipped (or dangerously equipped) cabin: a clearing, and in the middle of it an old mattress and two or three discarded car seats uprooted like pulled teeth. This man, in all likelihood, wasn't even Fennimore at all, but Fennimore's deranged uncle or older brother. She began to feel a dread which was both a fear of circumstances and a fear that she would not properly defend herself in fearful circumstances. Which she knew meant that her terror was taking on a social dimension and so was managing to convert itself, with no help from her, into the kind of humiliation that made her feel she almost had no right to ask, "Would there be a market or a little store nearby where I could perhaps just quickly pick up some fresh fruit or something?"

He said no. Everything closed, closed down at five.

Hysteria rose in her. Hunger was making her feel light-headed, deranged. She cried out in desperate (but small-voiced) outrage, "But I have to eat something! Isn't there a health food store somewhere around here that's still open? How can everything just shut down at five?"

Fennimore seemed to implode at this, wrenched the wheel hard left, then took off at a much greater clip through a series of streets and sidestreets that were curved or crooked. What was he doing? Heading even faster out of town, and by a confusing back way that she'd later never remember? They would get smashed up, and this was the very least of the bad things that would happen. "Where are we going?" she called out to him, trying to call out in a way that would not sound like crying out.

He shouted that they were going to a health food store—he did know of one place that might still be open. And very soon after this he did indeed make a violent turn into an alley where he had to slam on the brakes in order not to crash into a long collection of sheds not much bigger than cupboards.

He had parked behind what looked like the back of an old warehouse. He was furiously flushed and talking and breathing fast, his voice sour but urgent. "It's in there—it's called The Good Earth. Just walk down the plank between those two sheds and then hang a left. But make it snappy, we're working with an extremely tight schedule here."

She followed his directions and was surprised and above all intensely relieved to discover that the back of the shack she came into really *was* The Good Earth. She hurried along a dim aisle of vats and barrels to ask a girl down at the front for roasted sunflower seeds.

But the girl said that they were fresh out of the roasted. "We've got the raw, though."

But Marianne said she absolutely must have the roasted.

"You might try Herbie's Herbs, across the street and down that way just a wee bit. See the hanging sign with the tree on it?"

Marianne, out of breath, stood waiting for a chance to cross over to Herbie's Herbs. Cars drove by her with calm-looking people inside them. At last she was able to make her way through a clear space in the traffic and once she was inside Herbie's Herbs she shovelled a scoop of roasted sunflower seeds into a clear plastic sack. She was by now trembling with hunger, nearly tearful. She was also feeling frantic at the thought of keeping Fennimore waiting. If I don't hurry right back he'll be mad, she thought. She was feeling a bit dizzy, the armholes of her sleeveless blouse were limp with the damp of nervous perspiration. She pictured Fennimore drumming his fingers on his steering wheel, his face morbidly florid. He had lied to her too, telling her that everything closed down at five, and now she wasn't even able to find things, out of panic. The twist ties! She must be staring straight at them. Oh *there,* to the left of the spice jars. She reached one of them down and while she was twisting it around the neck of her little sack of seeds she remembered a story a friend had once told her, about a woman who'd accepted a drive from a man she had met at a picnic, and how when the driver refused to let her off at the corner of her street and had instead taken off at high speed for the highway, she'd opened his glove compartment and had methodically begun to float his bills and credit cards and postcards out the window—such a damning trail of identification that he'd had to skid to a stop, then throw himself out of his car at a run. And while he was running and stumbling along a deep ditch, cursing and searching like a bad giant in a fable for his lost possessions, the inventively methodical woman had fled. It occurred to Marianne that she must have been subconsciously recalling the clever-woman story while she was still in Fennimore's car because she now remembered that she'd noted that the door to his glove compartment had been removed, exposing a view of a roll of silver masking tape (wide enough to tape a mouth or a pair of eyes shut) and a heavy pair of pliers. Would she be able to make Fennimore slam on his brakes by tossing his pliers out the window? She didn't think so. But she simply must stop trying to frighten herself, the man was only unpleasant, after all, he was hardly a psychotic. And so she tried to think only practical thoughts. For instance, what else did she need? Yogurt! She hurried down to the wall of refrigerators at the back of the store, picked out a blueberry one, half-quart size, squinted up at the wall for plastic spoons. They'd be up at the front, but knowing this didn't keep her from peeking into each of the side aisles, just in case the spoons should magically appear. But no. And she should go to the organic fruit counter too, get herself an orange.

But the oranges looked battered and mouldy, and she instead picked out two nectarines. Her stomach was swarming with panic at the thought of how Fennimore's rage must be building out in the hot smelly car and so she said in a quick worried voice to the clerk up at the cash register, "Do you have any spoons?"

"Right here," said the young woman. Her eyes were shrewdly kind and she had poked what looked like ebony chopsticks into a chignon at the top of her springy fair hair. She reached to her left to extract a plastic spoon from a clutch of spoons that had been shoved into a pink pottery mug.

"Oh good," said Marianne. But she was feeling swimmy and damp up in the top of her own head, as if she might need to faint or throw up. "I'm in a bit of a hurry, actually, so I guess I'd better pay for these things quickly."

Her hands shook as she pulled the money out of her wallet, and when she glanced up she saw that the cashier was looking truly concerned for her. What a lovely kind face the young woman had! As if a life spent living in a small town had made her clairvoyant. Marianne felt a mad desire to say to her, "I think I might be in some kind of trouble, I wonder if you could advise me—"

But that's perfectly silly, said the prim voice of her upbringing. This Ray Fennimore writes a fine column on herbs for a health magazine, he's merely a bit cross with his wife because of the (much) aforementioned sit-down dinner, he's merely a bit of a passive aggressive, and she started to go toward the front door of the store so that she could cross the street to make her return to the other store and walk through its dim length to hurry back to the dusty back alley and Fennimore's car.

She had almost reached the big bins at the front when she turned back to the young woman. The thought struck her that God had arranged for her to be given a second chance, that God had arranged for The Good Earth to be strategically out of what she was wanting in order to get her beyond the magnetic field of Ray Fennimore and his toxic car and a darker fate. At this revelation, she spoke imploringly to the cashier. "I just realized something: I have to get to the bus station right away. Do you know where I could pick up a cab in a hurry?"

And the young woman called to her with a voice that seemed to sing out with pure rescue, "Turn left, run eight blocks, bus leaves at five-twenty! But it's sometimes a bit late! And there's usually two or three cabs at the front of the Embassy Hotel! A tall brick building! Painted red!"

Marianne breathlessly thanked her, then ran with a pain in her side all the way to the tall red hotel.

There was a black cab lying in wait there, long gleaming black panther, engine idling. Marianne pulled its door open and flung herself into the back seat. "The bus station!"

But the cabby, who had the calm flaxen fairness she had always associated with farm boys, seemed disoriented, sleep-deprived himself. And the early evening traffic was by this time barely moving. He shook his head, as if trying to clear it. And as he nosed the car out into the street he said, "This has not been my week."

Marianne was still feeling frantic, and even kept turning to look over her shoulder in paranoid terror, she was so afraid that Ray Fennimore's green station wagon might now be tailing the cab. Still, she felt compelled to ask the driver in a dry social voice, "What was so bad about it?"

The cabby said that he came from a good Christian family, and that he wasn't a bigot, or at least not to the extent that his daddy was. "He hates people who are gay. Me, I try to be tolerant. But these last few days, ninety per cent of my trade has been individuals of an alternative sexual persuasion."

Now they were trapped behind an army truck whose tied-on brown canvas roof made Marianne think of an evil prairie schooner. Why doesn't he try to pass it, she thought. And then: Is he gay himself? Is this what he's working his way up to confessing? Or maybe he thinks I am.

"So then last night this guy gets into my cab and I say to him, 'So how are you this fine evening?' And he—"

Now the military truck was moving very slowly ahead, almost asphyxiating them with its military fumes.

"Could we maybe try to get past these guys?"

"Got his blinkers on, but we should be able to shake him in a minute or two. Anyway, then this guy says to me, 'Totally shitty,' and so I go, 'Anything I can do to make you feel better?' And he goes, 'Thanks for the offer, buddy, but you just haven't got the sum of the parts,' and so then I decide that's *it*"—he slapped the steering wheel for effect as he said this—"I've *had* it, and I slam on the brakes and I go, 'Get outta my cab,' and he goes, 'Why? Because I'm *gay*?' and I go, 'No, because you're an *asshole*.'"

Gandee Falls, thought Marianne—town of short fuses, but now she could at last see the square-steepled yellow church with its four tiny black spires pointing up like four petrified wicks and so knew that they must be getting close to the depot. And now she could see worse: the bus she'd arrived on was just taking off, backing in its bland and stone-deaf way out of the station. She whimpered at the cabby, crying, "Please please please please *please* let me catch that bus," and tossing a ten-dollar bill at him, she pushed open the door and half fell onto the hard ground, but then right away stumbled up to run to the backing-up bus, banging with her crying fists on the doors until the driver let her in.

As the bus was moving out of town, Marianne dumped the sunflower seeds into the yogurt and then began to feed herself rapidly, wolfing down her food with the miniature spoon. In a rage beyond rage, Fennimore might manage to smash up all on his own, on the way home to his dinner. Was possibly even already dead or dying. She leaned back against the bristly plush of the bus seat and tried to feel guilt but couldn't seem to manage it. But then she also imagined a quite different scenario: she was driving out into the country with Fennimore and the trip was uneventful, but the evening at his house was a social embarrassment because he was barely bothering to take the time to talk to her about herbs, being too busy pouring glasses of wine for his friends. Then she pictured herself alone once again and standing on a deserted strip of highway just within sight of Fennimore's place (by now a Victorian stone mansion on a grim rise in a grove of dark trees) and this time she was waiting for the local bus into Gandee Falls but she kept having to step back whenever a car with a man wearing dark glasses would swerve in, its driver rolling down his window to call out and ask her if she was wanting a lift. But then another possibility occurred to her: Fennimore hadn't bothered to wait for her at all. Within five seconds of her disappearing into The Good Earth he was off.

That, she decided, is the real story. And she imagined herself telling it to a friend or to some of the people at work, a cautionary tale about her trip out into the deranged country, the short wild ride with the psychotic herbalist. She even had a punch line for it. A punch line that could double as a premonition. But it was a premonition that would come true only if she didn't allow herself to believe in it: That night she slept.

And in fact that night, after the children were in bed and she had taken the phone off the hook so that Fennimore couldn't call her up and accuse her, she did sleep, and with nothing to help her but a cup of Sleepytime Tea. She lay awake only long enough to recall the first few moments following her return home and how she had gone to the living-room doorway to ask her children if they'd been worried about her and how after a very long pause—the pause that it seemed to her all adolescent children must reserve for their parents (the pause in which they seem forever to be deciding that they might not have the strength to answer at all)—her oldest daughter, dressed all in black and sitting with one long booted black leg hanging over the arm of the big cane chair by the far window, had called out in an amused voice, "No! *Should* we have been?"

Toward morning Marianne dreamed that she was driving at a great clip through sunlit mountains on a crowded bus with no driver. Then she was in a car with a man who was an expert driver even though he seemed to be in a coma, he was so deeply asleep. A puffy calm sleeping man in a grey raincoat. She felt she must get him to wake up and so pulled at his sleeve until he opened his eyes. But once he was awake, he began to weave drunkenly, still infected by sleep—for a moment he was even Farley, but then she wasn't even with him any more, she was living in a tower with her three children, and then she was opening her bedroom window to see that there was a telephone hooked outside in the bright sunlight, on the outside brick wall of her neighbour's fifth-floor corner apartment. A phone that only a fireman could use. A fireman or an angel. "But how convenient," she said to herself, still lulled as she was by the impenetrable logic of the country of dreams.

THERE GOES THE
GROOM

COLD RAINY SPRING WITH TULIPS in tight bud late into May—all
of their tulip parts the same streamlined lizard green. It wasn't
until the middle of June that the days at last turned so bizarrely
southern that in the ravine at the end of the long park an army
of parasites began to spin a haze of what looked like white fur on
all the catkins. So that by the first day of summer whole groves
of leafy trees were bridal with poison blossoms.

But then summer hurried by, as summer will, was over in no
time, and one evening in the early fall I was standing dreaming
at the kitchen sink while I was rinsing teacups and saucers under
very hot water. Thinking of nothing. But then nothing was ever
nothing, whenever I thought I was thinking of nothing I was
always thinking of love, and after I'd finished shaking the drops
from the cups and was drying them I discovered that there was

something about the teacups' delicate warmth beaming through the tea-towel cloth that was making me imagine touching a man's face after I'd turned to him in bed in the dark. I had sexual thoughts often enough to make me feel lonely too, but there was nothing that could make me feel lonelier than this craving to touch a man's face. There were times when it could make me forget the world even more absolutely than thoughts of touching a man's body could. Or having a man crazy to touch my body. Sometimes when I was alone in the house and was carrying a basket of laundry up from the basement I'd even kiss and nuzzle the warm heap of pillowslips and shirts while at the same time I'd be feeling quite caressed myself, would feel as if a dry but warm hand had tucked a lock of my hair behind one of my ears while the hand's owner was looking into my eyes as if he could find the true answers to questions about tenderness there: Are you a serious person? Are you as serious about being with me like this as I need you to be?

But out in the real world, school was starting again and at the beginning of the second week of September there was a call from Mr. Dunphy, Tom's French teacher, wanting to let me know that Tom was skipping French class.

It was a windy wet afternoon and so before I went up to Tom's room I drew my cardigan out of the hall closet. It felt damp, as if it had a haze of dew on it from the rain, but I pulled it on anyway as I made my way up the stairs, and even buttoned it up primly before I knocked on Tom's door.

Then six quick little knocks, fierce and parental.

"What," said the trapped voice, sullen and wary.

"I need to talk to you for a minute."

"So?"

"So could I come in?"

"So you could come in."

I opened his door and went into his room and carefully sat on the end of his bed. But once I'd told him what Dunphy had said, he called me a failure.

"In what way?" I asked him. I spoke in a high warning voice. A precise voice. (Precise but frightened.) "At least be explicit," I said. "You can't call a person a failure and then not come up with even one single way in which that person *is* a failure. . . ."

He gazed at me. A long careful look that made me think of Norman—Norman arranging his objections in an orderly row so that he could begin one of his bracing and accusatory pep talks. It always surprised me when either of our children resembled their parents. Most of their childhood they had seemed to be so free of the taint of heredity. This made it all the more shocking to encounter, in a hitherto innocent arrangement of nose and eyes and mouth, a smile that could rise to a pair of eyes that had decided to turn against me. "Okay," he said. "You want me to be explicit, I'll be explicit—I consider you a total failure as a human being, is that explicit enough for you?"

My throat was all at once in so much pain that I had to leave him and go into my own room and sit down on my bed. I was in despair, not only about this moment, but about the future, the future as endless present, exactly like this present I was living through now. I looked at my untidy bedroom and saw it as an untidy bedroom in a too tiny (and too untidy) rented house. I looked at the wet window and was glad it wasn't sunny because sun always seemed, if I was feeling sad, infinitely sadder than rain. I gazed in a dull way down at the scatter of pencils and spilled pennies and bus tickets and a jar of Tiger Balm and a stump of pink lipstick rolled to a stop at the heel of a shoe, and I thought: And things won't get better.

But the next morning already there was a reprieve, and we lived through the following three weeks calmly enough, no reproaches, meeting mainly for meals, all of us busy out in the world. At least until the afternoon I came home to hear Tom out in the kitchen banging the cast-iron frying pan onto the stove. Before I'd even hung up my jacket, he was wailing at me, "Where's the mustard, for fuck's sake? And don't you think we should at least *try* to get some organization in this crummy hellhole? We're out of butter too, Mum! And there's this bowl of really mouldy guck at the back of the fridge. . . ."

Bruno, sitting at the dining-room table and cutting out a pink cardboard lion for a project at school, seemed to hate both of us. He dropped his scissors onto the floor and then scooped them up and in a rage pelted them at the sofa. "Why is everybody always yelling in this house?" he yelled. "Why can't a person ever get any peace?" And he stamped up the stairs in a fury and slammed his bedroom door.

Much later that night, when the house was quiet and Tom and Bruno were up in their beds and (I hoped) sound asleep, I dragged a garbage bag over to the fridge and scooped wilted things into it, feeling ashamed. I found bewildering items in clouded but once-clear plastic bags: a zucchini squash, its insides gone liquidly soft; a mildewed onion. Also two plastic containers of yogurt, never opened until now and growing grey fur. And iceberg lettuce in a forgotten brown paper bag and of such ancient vintage that it was leaking a fetid caramel-coloured sauce. I remembered that there was no system to my housework, no rules to keep down the dirt. Take the way I'd let anyone at all clomp into the main part of the house in big winter boots, the broken-off segments of slush-tread turning the kitchen floor muddy and repellent.

Hills of oranges backed hills of tomatoes, the tomatoes almost translucent in the hot fall sunshine. Beyond the fruit stalls, boxed-in small fields of red tulips. And beyond the tulips, sorting efficiently through a basket of apples, a sharp-faced but pretty grey-haired woman in mannish black slacks and a short-sleeved silk shirt the same red as the flowers. Bruno and Tom came to stand with quiet urgency beside me—they all at once seemed tall, quiet and tall—and then Tom whispered that the woman in the red shirt was a former girlfriend of Norman's. A woman named Dorie. He said in a low voice, "We'll go get the salami and meet you out at the deli."

I pretended to assess the tomatoes while I studied the woman picking out apples. She finally chose three and was then ready to walk fatly and briskly away. The leather strap of her handbag (bumping on her left hip) and the leather strap of her camera case (bumping on her right hip) gave her a dark leather X across her silky and competent back.

The lawyer, Douglas Walcott, was only in his late twenties, but above his pebbled red necktie he had adultly sorrowful eyes. Older man's eyes and an older man's tie. His fingers played on the raised silk pebbles as if they were the buttons on an unhappy accordion, and while I was telling him that I didn't personally want anything from my husband, all I wanted was fair child support for as long as my children were living at home, he watched me shrewdly, doubtfully.

Outside the tall windows, Ottawa stretched far below us, tiny and shining city. I told Walcott that when I'd told my husband I was going to begin divorce proceedings against him, he had surprised me by asking, "Why can't things just stay as they are?"

"Are you sure your husband is not still hoping for a reconciliation?"

"Oh, no—I am sure he is not."

"But if he won't give you the house and you don't get any money, what's to become of you?"

"I do have a job," I primly reminded him.

"But you've already told me it doesn't pay very well. And isn't it only a part-time job? Didn't you say so yourself?"

"Yes."

"And so why won't you take whatever help you can get?"

"Because I want to be free of him."

"And if he sells the house?"

"Then I'll get a share of the profits—"

"Half, surely. That's what you're entitled to."

"Yes. But not quite half. More like a third, I think."

"Why is that?"

"Because he put some of his own money into it. He used his own money to build an apartment down in the basement and then we rented it out—"

"His own money?" he asked me sharply. "In what way?"

"Money he had to borrow. From his mother."

I could see him turning this over in his mind and feeling contempt for my husband—even more contempt than the contempt he must have felt he was required to feel as my legal adviser. But then he rallied, frowned down at my file. "And you've worked where else? In a library. But not as a librarian, I gather. And in an art gallery out west, but that was years ago. And as a receptionist for a dentist, but that was only for a little over a year. And besides, none of these jobs could be called a trade or a profession. And so my advice to you is to go for the house. Failing that, you should most certainly get some kind of help. . . ."

"You don't think I'll be able to manage on my own?" I asked him, and I was shocked to hear how flirty my voice sounded. I was even smiling a little as I decided to ask him an even more dangerous question, I even held my right hand pressed to my heart to ask it: "Do I look to *you* like a person who will *fail?*"

He blushed, and so I had my terrible answer.

I could feel myself blushing too. But I was also all at once determined to show him—to show everyone—what a grand success I could be.

But at that same moment he stood. "I want you to get something, some kind of protection. In case things don't always go well for you. . . ." Then he asked me to step out into the hall for a minute or two. "I'd like to introduce you to my senior partner."

I followed him out into the hallway and then waited while he went into an office with C. Miller MacLeod painted on its door. I could hear their lowered voices, part of a phrase now and then. From the older lawyer, not Walcott. I heard the older voice say ". . . talk some sense into her . . ." and as a sort of depressing background music to the older lawyer's voice I kept hearing Walcott's voice saying over and over: in case things don't always go well for you, in case things don't always go well for you, in case things don't always go well for you. . . . But then the older voice came closer and a door opened and C. Miller MacLeod stepped out into the hall, his eyes bright with inquiry as he said in a Scots voice, "Good day, Mrs. Gradzik."

We shook hands. But I found myself feeling ill at ease under the clinical brutality of his gaze. He said, "I suppose you might marry again." But his eyes seemed to say he doubted it. And then he asked me how old I was, if I didn't mind his asking.

"Thirty-nine."

"That old!" He gazed at me with a mournful candour. "Statistically, the chances are against it then."

My face burned as I boarded the elevator and then sank to the street. And when I described my feelings to my friend Deedee the next day at work I told her I'd walked away from that place wanting to enact the whole scene all over again, told her I'd wanted to speak to C. Miller MacLeod in a cold entertained voice, told her I'd wanted to tell him that I considered myself to be above and beyond statistics. "I wanted to yell at him, 'What in the name of God have statistics got to do with *me*?'"

Deedee was stapling piles of notes together, but she looked up at me to say, "'Everything!' God yelled back at Kristina Gradzik."

When Tom and Bruno came home after seeing a movie with Norman the following Sunday night, the first thing Bruno said to me was, "Dad has a new girlfriend."

I asked him what she was like.

"She wears big earrings and she laughs a lot."

Tom glanced at Bruno, then turned to me. His gaze was both cynical and imploring. "Yeah," he said. "She's really nervous too. You get so you want to tell her to stuff a sock in her mouth or something."

But Bruno seemed to be lost in some infatuated dream. He said, "Her earrings are *immense*." He looked feverish, exhausted. He said, "What are those things that little kids are always running behind with a stick? You know—in nursery rhymes. . . ."

"Oh yeah," said Tom. "Hoops."

I had a question, too. "Did Dad tell you her name?"

Tom said he did. "But now I can't remember it."

Bruno looked up from the book he was reading. Or was pretending to read. "I remember it," he whispered. "Her name is Elaine."

My divorce hearing was set for early November. Norman would not need to put in an appearance, Walcott said. But I should bring along a friend for moral support. I asked Deedee if she could come with me, and she said she could. But she made it clear that she was in total agreement with Walcott: Please don't be a masochist, please try to get yourself something, please don't be a fool.

Walcott called me the night before I was to go to the courthouse. "I have just one last request. One last thing I want you to do for yourself. I want you to ask your husband to give you a dollar a year. It's vital that you get it, especially in circumstances such as yours. Because what it'll mean is we can haul him into court if ever you should have the misfortune to find yourself ill or destitute. We'll have some claim on him. And if he won't willingly help you, we can garnishee his wages. So give him a call tonight and ask him to meet you at court tomorrow morning so he can tell the judge he'll pay you the annual dollar."

I said I would. I was all at once beginning to suspect that Walcott had been right all along and that my future was quicksand. I pictured a dollar with the pale-green queen on it and I felt afraid.

I called Norman first thing after supper. But he wouldn't commit himself on the phone. "I'll meet you tomorrow morning at the courthouse. On my way to work." And it seemed to me that he said the word "work" as if only he—in all of the work-addicted Western world—truly knew what real work was.

But then he had something else to tell me. He'd had a letter from my mother, a response to his news that we were getting divorced. "A letter of support" was how he described it, a letter from Loo—because that's what he called her—telling him that I was a hard person and that she sent him her love.

I said, "What a bitch."

Yes, he said in a sober but contented voice—he, too, had been somewhat taken aback by it. "It was fairly savage," he said. "About you, my darling. Not that I didn't agree with ninety per cent of it."

"What I want to know is, did it make you think less of Loo?"

"To tell you the truth, my darling, I never thought all that much of Loo in the first place."

Winter was already on its way the next morning, the darkish early November morning of my divorce, and the upstairs hallway was cold but steamy from everyone's shower. I stared out at the dim day as I pulled on my most narrow black skirt, my black nylons. The blouse I buttoned myself into was a pink silk with weakened pleats in its sleeves. I fitted my feet into my old gold party pumps—the ones that looked as if they'd had Celtic designs tattooed on their toes. They were utterly wrong, anyone could see that, but I did not have the energy to kick them off and work my feet into more appropriate footgear. My head hurt me, and while I was brushing my hair my eyes started to fill. I didn't feel sad, only a bit sick and dizzy. I felt I must concentrate very hard in order not to disgrace myself in some unprecedented way in the courtroom.

Deedee was waiting for me in the downstairs corridor of the courthouse on a long churchy oak pew—the only calm one in a long row of quietly desperate strangers. Her lips were chapped, lipstickless. She had pulled on one of her husband's old parkas and was wearing her hair loose and her Navajo earrings. She didn't seem to be entirely awake yet. I was so grateful to her for getting up early to come to be with me that I whispered, "I don't know how I'll ever be able to thank you for everything."

Out of the side of her mouth she said, "Don't go getting all emotional now—Norman'll see you. He's here already, he just went to get himself a coffee."

Norman came along the hallway at that very moment, looking as if he'd had to stop and lean his head against a tree on his way to the courthouse and throw up. He spoke coldly to Deedee, as if he despised her for being his wife's loyal friend. Then he turned his cold attention to me. "You're the one who wanted the clean break," he told me. "And so there won't be any dollar." He stood for a moment, holding the empty paper cup in his hand. His tiepin was stuck into an expensive silk tie the dull pink of a snout. It made him look elegant, adenoidal. He looked like a man who would always be dapper. He crushed his paper cup in one hand, poked it into a pocket. "It's better for you this way, believe me."

Then he fled down the hallway.

The atmosphere in the courtroom seemed to me to be the atmosphere of a solemn nightmare—the air charged with a kind of well-bred, nervous shame. And even though the court clerk read out a document that proclaimed that my husband had said I was a good mother and would be the one to be getting the custody of the children, I bowed my head as if he had read out the opposite.

Once I had got my decree nisi, I could tell that Deedee was in a fury about the dollar all over again, because after we'd closed the courtroom's heavy door behind us, she yanked her parka hood rebukingly up.

In an attempt to appease her, I tried a little joke. "Decree nisi. Sounds Japanese."

She stared straight ahead.

"This corridor smells exactly like the corridors in my old high school. Marble halls and Dustbane."

No response. Only the sound of our footsteps, walking fast.

"Don't worry about Norman not helping me out. If ever I'm in any kind of real trouble, he'll help me out, I know he will. . . ."

"You can say it, friend, I don't have to believe it."

"He'll give me a lecture, but he'll also give me the money. . . ."

Her not answering was like footsteps:

no answer

no answer

no answer

no answer

We opened another heavy door and stepped out into the city's arctic air and the wind tore at us. Even inside my heavy winter coat I could feel it nosing its way up my bloated silk sleeves. But now Deedee was talking again, now she was saying that what was really dumber than dumb was for lawyers to ask ex-husbands to give their ex-wives a dollar a year. What man wouldn't smell a rat, she said, when all he had to pay his ex-wife was one pathetic little dollar? Why not make it a sum that didn't sound like a scam? But then she seemed to tire of the subject because what she said next was, "Let's go to one of the little cafés down by the market, get ourselves some hot soup," and so we left her car where it was and walked fast toward Rideau Street, into the tearful wind.

Summer sounds tinkled in the clear winter air—wind chimes knocking against one another in the polar breeze of the entrance to the café we settled on—and after the waitress had brought us our soup, Deedee tore open a croissant and mashed butter into it, shoved half of it into her mouth, then painfully swallowed it to say, "You know what you should be doing? You should be thinking of ways to keep the wolf from the door. . . ." And then she told me that I reminded her of a parable. "Or is it a fable? You know the one. The one about the grasshopper and the cricket. Isn't it the cricket who only wants to have a good time? And then ends up dying of starvation in the middle of a blizzard?"

"I don't only want to have a good time," I said. I hardly even want to have a good time at *all,* I thought. I spread my cold fingers out over the steam from my soup. But I knew that I also loved money, or at least loved the things that money could buy. Loved money—not to hoard, but to squander. Knew that if I had money I'd become an out-of-control spendthrift. Knew that I loved embroidered batiste blouses and exquisite underthings in plum silk and peach silk, knew that I loved rare scents and creams. I pictured a tall-windowed room furnished with rugs that were expensively threadbare, historic, a room equipped with a low fire and flowers, a lovely red room with low-hung and small gloomy landscapes that would announce my unassuming and perfect good taste. And yet at the same time that I was longing for the glamour of money, I was also longing for the glamour of poverty. I longed for poverty the way I longed for pain at the dentist's. I wanted it to happen, and to happen quickly, because once it happened it would be over and done with, and then I wouldn't be in pain any more. And yet I knew that this was flawed thinking; dental pain was brief pain, and poverty pain was long pain—poverty pain just kept compounding itself, like a bank certificate's interest. "I do worry," I said. "I worry all the time." But then I only found myself thinking of how happy I was to make my escape from my marriage and of the way that Norman, at family gatherings, used to too easily be persuaded to get up to make a little speech. Not quite an endless little speech, but quite endless enough. How smug he used to look then, his eyes closed as he basked in the sound of his own platitudes, feeding on them. And then I remembered the way, when he had to get up at night to go to the bathroom, he would pull on his socks and then tuck his pyjama legs into them. How diabolically methodical that had seemed to me to be. I was jealous, I suppose, because I was too impulsive to bother to kick my feet into my slippers and so would invariably choose to run over the chilly floors barefoot and come down with a cold.

I told Deedee about the letter my mother had sent to Norman, and about the way Norman called my mother Loo. "But then she's always adored him, he's her kind of guy. And do you know what else? The whole time he was telling me about her letter he kept calling me 'my darling.'"

"Bet he'll keep in touch with her after the divorce," said Deedee, narrowing her eyes to look out at the bright windy street. "Send her little presents, little love notes, he's the type. Anything to make *you* look bad, my darling—"

I smiled at her. I was feeling expansive. "And what do you think these little love notes will say?"

"Oh, they'll be profound," she said airily. "'Dearest Loo, how are *you?*'"

We laughed, and I found myself thinking how really enjoyable it was, getting divorced. It was pleasant. This whole lunch was pleasant. It seemed to me that Deedee and I had never before had such a pleasant conversation.

But now Deedee was quoting someone, some futurologist she'd heard on her car radio on her way to the courthouse. "And according to him, things will only get worse and worse: war, famine, pestilence."

The pleasant day blew away.

"Don't be a fool," said Deedee. "And please don't sit there looking so phoney and noble—it doesn't become you. . . ."

But she was wrong about me. I believed in the worst, always, and always believed it would happen to me. Or did I? Didn't I also believe just the opposite? Whenever I tried to answer a magazine quiz about personality types I always scored high for opposing qualities. I was an optimist, but also a pessimist. I had a great need for solitude, but I was also an extrovert. I was poorly organized, but also a compulsive. "Don't worry so much," I said, and as I said it I was struck by how much I sounded like Tom and Bruno when they were about to do some ill-advised thing. I even went so far as to say what they always said: "Everything will be fine."

After we'd closed ourselves into the stale cold of Deedee's car she asked me if Norman had a girl.

"The boys say he does—a hyperactive woman whose name is Elaine."

Snow started to fall heavily just before noon on New Year's Eve, and by four-thirty the storm had been upgraded to a blizzard. While Tom was over at the stove making himself cocoa, I stood at the kitchen window feeding myself pretzels and looking out at the big wind in the trees. I remembered making cocoa for myself when I was a child—the pleasure of lifting the wrinkled disk of grey cocoa skin up from the top of the steaming hot cocoa with a fork.

Then it was time to bring the leftover goose and cold cooked apples and prunes out to the round table in the living room. Tom and I served everything onto the heavy blue-leafed pottery plates and then I called Bruno.

He came to the table with a riddle for us. "What did Napoleon keep up his sleevies?"

We tried to guess, but we couldn't.

"His armies!"

"Moaning and gnashing of teeth," said Tom. But I suspected he'd be brooding about it all through the meal. And, sure enough, while I was serving the apple cake with one of the silver spatulas I'd been given as a bride, he tilted back in his chair to say to Bruno, "Okay, Herr Gradzik. Okay, mein Herr, vhat did Napoleon keep opp his sleevies?"

"Apart from his armies?"

"Ja."

Bruno looked over at me. But I had to tell him that I was no good at these things.

"Do you give up?"

We gave up.

"His Elbas."

"That's extremely clever, Tom."

Bruno said, "I don't get it."

Tom told him the story of Napoleon's years of exile. "For a while he was on the island of Elba, but then he was exiled to the island of Ste. Hélène. And that's where he died, isn't it, Mum? On the island of Ste. Hélène?"

"One of the two, but I'm not sure which one."

Tom wanted to know if it was just old age that he died from.

"I think they think now that he may have been poisoned. It seems to me that I read somewhere that they dug up his body and the whole corpse was green. . . ." And again I thought of the green queen on the dollar.

The next day, just before lunch, Norman came to pick the boys up for New Year's brunch and a movie, and I spent the afternoon washing my hair and going to the living-room window every twenty minutes or so. What was I looking for? I didn't know. The house seemed tauntingly empty, but ordinarily this emptiness wouldn't have bothered me at all; ordinarily I'd be overjoyed to have the place all to myself—ordinarily there would be so many things I'd want to do, left to my own devices: narcissistic, self-indulgent private things. I could make love to myself or read from the book I kept hidden under the sweaters up in my sweater drawer—a wine paperback with raised silver letters that looked quilted, bloated, and on its back cover two bold silver questions: A DARK PERVERSION? OR IMAGINATIVE LOVE PLAY? I could even wander around the house in the nude if I felt so inclined—something I could never do when the boys were at home—or turn the radio up loud and dance to it. But I didn't seem to want to do any of these things, I seemed to expect myself to be incredibly ladylike, to set a good example to myself for the new year.

Tom and Bruno came back just after dark. They clomped into the house, pushing and poking at one another, buoyed up by some joke they had just told or been told, and as they lunged past me, Tom said in a low voice, "All systems on alert, Madam Mother—the Father is coming in to have a brief word with you. . . ." And then I could hear the two of them tramping up the stairs and snickering to each other, as if the words "the Father" and "brief word" could not possibly belong in the same conversation. But their warning made me scuttle up the stairs right behind them to fix myself up—not for Norman, but just so he wouldn't be able to tell himself I looked drab. I could already hear him neatly kicking the snow off his boots—six precise little taps against the outside lower doorstep. I breathlessly peered at myself in the tall mirror in the upper hallway and saw that my blouse was lopsided. I tucked it back into my trousers and brushed my hair fast but then took my time going back down the stairs.

Norman was already standing in the centre of the living room and was sheepishly smiling up at me as I came walking down. He had grown his beard again and it was now so curly and black it made him look darkly cherubic. Night snow sparkled in it. He heeled off his overshoes. "Kris, I wanted to speak to you privately for a moment."

"Fine," I said in a cool voice. "Go right ahead."

He took off his coat, then went to hang it up in the vestibule, and as he came back into the living room again I couldn't help thinking: How handsome he looks! In his pale-lilac shirt! And his tie. He had always had such an instinct for picking the really stunning ones. This one was in muted army and mud colours, a new variation on one of the old hand-blocked designs.

"Kris—I'm getting married again."

I was amazed, and to hide my amazement I quickly said, "Is her name Elaine?"

But the question seemed to make him uneasy. He said, "Her name is Dorie."

"Oh," I said. And then: "I think Tom and Bruno pointed her out to me at the market once. She was buying apples—"

His left eye seemed to flinch at this, seemed to say: Naturally you would want to be ironical. Out of bitterness—or out of envy perhaps—but I'm the one who's getting married again, I'm the one life will get better for.

I asked him when the actual ceremony was to be.

"On the sixteenth of June. Then we'll be going to Europe for three weeks. Dorie has relatives over in Scotland, and one of her Scottish uncles owns a place down in Spain. . . ."

I wondered if he was at all remembering our own time in Spain, two weeks in a little town called Palamos. On the Costa Brava.

"He barely even uses the damn thing and so she's free to borrow it any time she wants to. A hacienda, I suppose you could call it. On the Costa Brava. . . ."

I wanted to ask him more questions. Which was odd, because ordinarily I couldn't wait for him to go. Ordinarily his going would fill me with the most wonderful euphoria. And ordinarily Norman, sensing how much I really wanted him to go, would inflict his presence on me just a little bit longer. He would pull on his coat, but then think of some other quick thing he needed to tell me. He would hesitate in the vestibule, then come back into the living room again and take off his coat. And yet he would look very serious as he opened up a whole new area for discussion, as if the last thing in the world he wanted to do was thwart me. But this time, sensing how much my curiosity was aroused—how much I wanted him to stay, for once—he seemed eager to be off.

I stood at the window and watched the military swing of the squared shoulders of his black coat as he walked down the snow-packed path to the corral where his car was parked.

There goes the groom.

(I was trying to get my euphoria back.)

But footsteps were coming down the dark stairs behind me. It was Tom. As he passed by me, he said in a low voice, "Maybe

it's better for you not to stand at the window right now, Mum—
Dorie might see you. She came in the car with him."

"Oh," I said, startled. And I stepped fast to one side, hid
myself behind the protective weave of the curtain. But from my
new vantage point I could still watch Norman's headlights backing bumpily away in the clear winter night.

I could hear Tom out in the kitchen too, making himself
toast, the rasp of the knife over the dry toasted bread.

I walked down to the kitchen, stood for a moment in the
doorway. "Thanks for telling me not to stand at the window."

He said sure, no problem.

"Did Dad tell you his news? That he's planning to marry
Dorie?"

"So *that's* it. All afternoon I could tell he had some big thing
up his sleeve."

"Opp his sleevies?"

But neither of us laughed.

"Apparently Dorie has an uncle who owns a place over in
Spain, on the Costa Brava, half the time he doesn't even
bother to use it, so maybe you and Bruno'll get a chance to
stay there some time when Dad and Dorie are over there on
vacation."

"Big deal," Tom, with dark loyalty, answered.

But in the end he would want to go, it would be only human
to want to go to Spain, Bruno would want to go too, and I pictured my two sons stretched out on a long and spectacular beach
on the Costa Brava, two young men by the ocean, growing
away from me even as they were sunbathing, and possibly even
sunbathing on the same beach Norman and I had christened our
own little beach, half an hour from Palamos and so long ago, one
of the instructive little tricks irony would play with time and

geography. Or at the very least they would lie on that same Spanish coast and under that same Spanish sun.

But then I saw the ocean as a darker ocean, more Swedish than Spanish, and a plump-thighed Dorie was awkwardly dispensing food from a basket, and the conversation she was trying to keep alive with Tom and Bruno was overly polite, trivial, and Norman was making strained and obvious little jokes, and the boys didn't even want to be in Spain in the first place, they only wanted to be back at home with their friends.

But I wondered if Deedee had really meant it when she'd called me a masochist, and after a few moments I went up to my room and slid open the drawer where I kept the book on sado-masochism hidden. I had underlined something in it, months ago, a line or two in an excerpt from a book called *Eros, The Meaning of My Life,* and now I wanted to see what it was that I had found so thrilling. I found the underlined lines almost at once, and although it seemed to me now that they weren't all that shocking, or at least not all that shocking when compared with so much of the rest of the book (I realized that I'd been expecting and even dreading words that would convey some brutal pleasure anticipated), a quick glance told me that they still had the power to make me feel shame: "I felt the stimulus powerfully in my private parts. I felt the pulse beat of my raging blood hammering in my vulva. I felt close to fainting and almost threatened to sink to the floor, overpowered by the excitement. . . ." And as I stood reading them again it occurred to me that they must have evoked feelings from deepest childhood—the almost unbearable sexual excitement of a game I had played with my brothers when we had all been so young that we hadn't called the game Husband and Wife but Father and Mother.

But I had no sooner fitted the book back into its drawer than I was imagining these particular words being lifted out of context—someone was reading them aloud to someone—and I was all at once afraid of how laughable they (and therefore I) would seem, and at this same moment I made myself imagine myself old—perhaps ill, perhaps destitute; I might even be dying or was even possibly already (newly) dead, and Tom and Bruno were going through my "effects." Because wasn't that what people's possessions were called, after they were dead? Their effects? The effects that would, one way or another, affect others? I saw one son, then the other son, pick up my clandestine book. I saw them reading the damning words—*raging, hammering, vulva*—I saw them exchange a bewildered look. But is this possible? Our little mother?

Of course I could see to it that this didn't happen, could carry the book down to the garbage can this very minute, could shove it deep down under four or five hats of grapefruit, the toppled earthy damp mounds of coffee grounds, crushed eggshells. And if even that didn't feel like protection enough, I could do worse: tear off the cover, tear the quilted silver letters into bloated silver bits, rip out all the pages, pour coffee down on them, smear them with jam.

But I couldn't do it, I didn't want to throw the book away, I was attached to it, I planned to read it again.

I instead went into the bathroom to look at myself in the mirror. I wanted to see what my face would have to tell me. I thought: So it's really over then, something final has happened. But I knew I shouldn't lie to myself. From now on, there would be complications. From now on, whenever Norman brought the boys home after dinner and a movie there would always be the possibility of another face there, and Norman walking that tightrope between the two faces. The face in the house. The face in the car window. I saw it as lost and white, watching me from the other side.

INVISIBLE TARGET

MY FIRST YEAR AT THE HOSPITAL I wrote long letters home. The people in my family got into fights if we didn't play word games—in the car, at the dinner table—and so I hoped that my parents would be entertained by the fine use the student nurses had made of the supervisor on Male Surgery, a terrifying woman whose name was Miss Poole. "When we were studying for the anatomy and physiology exams," I wrote home in early October of my first year in training, "the words SOME CLASSMATES HAVE UNDERESTIMATED RUTHLESS CALLOUS MISS POOLE were the keys to remembering the first letters we needed for the bones on our list." And then I named the bones:

scapula
clavicle
humerus

ulna
radius
carpals
metacarpals
phalanges

The voyeurism that medical people can so easily indulge in must have appealed to us too—the fact that we now had the right (and even the duty) to ask impertinent questions of total strangers. "Have you had a bowel movement?" we were instructed to ask the patients as we made our morning rounds, taking their pulses and checking for fevers. Or, more discreetly, "Have you had a B.M.?" We also learned, as children learn skipping songs from older children, medical jokes and ditties that were passed down to us from the student nurses who were one class ahead of us, and after we'd been told that a post-mortem was never called a post-mortem but was instead called a P.M., we chanted up and down the hallways of the first-year dorm:

If you don't have a B.M.
In the P.M.,
You'll have a P.M.
In the A.M.

As for the patients, the ones who were our favourites were the ones who would have been our favourites out in the world—the ones who were at least as fascinated by us as we were by them. The unfortunate others—the ones who catered too hysterically to their afflictions, the ones who saw us as mere functionaries of mercy and so didn't even bother to learn our names, the ones who bleated out the generic "Nurse! Nurse!"—

were the ones we gave short shrift to. We were as hard-hearted in our dealings with them as even the most arrogant of the senior nurses would have been. Possibly even more hard-hearted, in the impatience of being young. Although there were so many hardened older nurses in that hospital it would have been nearly impossible to outdo them in coldness. I often felt it would be taking your life in your hands to be sick in such a place, and the more I didn't ever want to be a patient there, the more I didn't want to be a nurse. But I still wasn't able to make up my mind to pack up and leave. I was waiting for something, for some unspeakable horror that I could hold up to the light to prove to myself—to myself and others (and by others I can only imagine that I meant my mother)—that the hospital was a truly monstrous place.

Due to alphabetical accident, my name (Linda Bishop) happened to immediately precede Jennifer Breithaupt, and because Breithaupt had changed her mind about becoming a nurse and so had never turned up, I was the only probationer on the ground floor of the student residence who didn't have someone to room with. I had mixed feelings about this; the part of me that was hysterically modest was even intensely relieved—I had been dreading the thought of unhooking my brassiere to let my breasts spill out in front of a stranger, or doing a shy squirm to work my way out of my underpants. But I couldn't help feeling desperately homesick as I sat alone in my room every night at bedtime—not homesick for home, but homesick for the hilarious dormitory life I'd pictured before I'd *left* home. I would sit on the bed that stood next to the made-up white bed that had no probationer to sleep in it and try not to eavesdrop on the cheerful insults people were yelling out to each other down at the far end of the hallway, insults that were invariably followed by shrieks and the elated sounds of bedroom doors being slammed rudely shut. All around me, those first weeks, student nurses hurried off to classes or down to the cafeteria or out to the movies in small laughing groups of threes and fours and it was soon apparent that their best friends were their roommates. But no, it wasn't soon apparent at all—it was only eventually apparent; in the beginning I didn't experience the friendships that were forming all around me as situational, I was much too lonely to see them as that, I only saw them as yet more damning evidence that I was by nature an outcast.

But early in October I learned that I too would get a roommate. Her name was Holly Bostwick and she was said to be the daughter of a United Church minister from a small town near Sackville. Picturing someone wren-like and plain, I felt the panic of impending guilt by association—felt that now, instead of being an outcast on my own (which was just barely bearable), I would become part of an unlucky team and we would be outcasts together and this would somehow be a thousand times worse. But then the rumours began to fly, and in no time at all everyone knew Holly's story because she was being admitted to the school five weeks late and bits and pieces of her sexual history were kept very busy preceding her. It turned out that some of the probationers had brothers who'd known her at Acadia, or brothers or cousins who'd heard news of her escapades at dances at Dal. She was wild, it was said. No, she was worse than wild, she was *bad*.

We were assembling enema trays to bring to the bedsides of seven rubber dummies the Thursday afternoon the teaching supervisor brought Holly Bostwick into the practice room. I was astounded by her appearance, she was so gentle looking. Her hair was hazy, angelic, and her pale lips were in some kind of pain all on their own, they were so voluptuous and sad. She was still in her street clothes—a black tartan skirt and black blazer—and it turned out that she not only had a complicated sexual history, she also had an ailment (syphilis) to go with it. I didn't hear this from her directly, but from someone else. All I ever heard from her directly was that once a week she had to go down to see the residence doctor for a shot of penicillin and a "little chat."

Until Holly Bostwick's arrival, I had been called Bish. But now I was rechristened Bitch and we were a duo: Boss and Bitch. Did we mind this? When the last thing Boss was was bossy? And when I wasn't a bitch? Although secretly I thought (and even hoped) that I sometimes could be. But the joke that was implied in the nicknames was that they didn't suit. They were like the secret names we gave to certain doctors: "Tiny" for one of the towering surgeons, "Flash" for Dr. Gordon, a shuffling old urologist who refused to retire.

Or we were called B and B. Which naturally led to our being called Bed and Breakfast. "Hey, Bed!" people would yell after us, hurrying to catch up. "Hey, Breakfast! Wait up for us!" But in this case there was more of an attempt to be accurate: Boss was Bed, I was Breakfast. Not that we got close. But then Boss didn't get close to anyone else at the hospital either—she even seemed, in the dreamy way she went about her work on the wards, to be on another planet. On loan, so to speak, from the world of sex. Because of the syphilis she was under curfew, and so had to be in residence every night by ten-thirty, but very soon after her arrival, there were fresh rumours and according to these fresh rumours she spent the early part of most evenings at a private men's club down on Union Street. Shirley Fielding, the probie who told me this, also told me that Boss had sex with the men in the club, but because of the syph she kept her underpants on. She said in a low voice, "And you and I both know that that's a really dirty thing to do."

But I didn't know, I didn't even know what she was talking about. But I should try to defend Boss, I thought. She is my roommate, after all. And yet I didn't know how to defend her when I didn't understand what it was she'd done wrong.

And so I only watched her. But there was nothing to learn, at least not from her: she was neat, she was quiet, she was efficient, she was in and out. But mostly out. Was she even intelligent? It was not a question it would have occurred to me to ask. I only felt what I think everyone felt: she was lovely, she was living a life of mystery, it was enough.

I invited Boss home for the Thanksgiving weekend. I was sure my mother would approve of her, she so adored well-mannered young women, especially pretty ones. It rained on the morning we set out, it even rained the whole time we were chugging across the Bay of Fundy on the boat, and after we'd disembarked at Digby, we caught the Wolfville train in a slightly warmer rain, then sat gazing self-consciously out at cows in damp meadows and, beyond them, at the rain-darkened back sheds and back gardens of settlements, tiny towns. Boss's eyebrows had a singed look, and she was wearing her boxy pleated black tartan skirt and a tailored pink shirt with a black necktie, leftover military clothes from her depraved boarding school days. We had by this time run out of things to talk about, and so had turned our attention to the landscape—had been reduced to looking out at the wet fields with such sad concentration that anyone passing by us would have had to conclude that our feelings had been hurt.

Perhaps the middle-aged man who'd been eyeing us off and on ever since Digby had concluded that too, for he got to his feet and stood swaying a little, beside us, in the aisle. Then he sat heavily down on our side of the train, doing a parody of a man squeezing himself into a bashful pigeon-toed triangle to make himself small enough to fit in between two voluptuous women. Even though he was really only sitting next to me. A ruse designed to give him a better view of Boss. Or so I thought. But it turned out that he was willing to give us equal attention. I was wearing a low-cut green sweater, and his eyes kept moving from what he could see of my breasts to Boss's bare knees and then back to my breasts again. He had wiry grey hairs in his nostrils and his voice was squeaky and breathy. When he discovered that we were getting off the train at Wolfville he said, "You girls not worried about getting wet in the rain? Because it just so happens that I've got my truck parked in Wolfville, just behind the station. Give you a lift to wherever you're going—"

I quickly said, "No, we're not worried. Someone's coming to pick us up."

The someone was my mother. Tightly tied into her fashionable grey poplin raincoat, she was waiting for us on the railway platform, as tensely attractive as ever. Even the breathy man seemed to think so; seemed to inhale her as he hurried by her, then guiltily waggled a hand at Boss and me, as if he'd recently said something awful about us to someone and was afraid we would somehow be able to guess what it was.

And my mother did adore Boss, walked arm in arm with her on our way out of the station, and after lunch took the two of us for a boringly eternal drive out into the country, after having insisted that Boss sit up in the front with her, be her own special friend. Brooding and alone on the back seat, I was forced to face the fact that I'd hoped to gain in glamour by bringing home such a calmly glamorous friend. But my plan had backfired, as my plans (whenever they involved my mother) so frequently had a tendency to do. And so I sat glumly hunched in my corner and stared out at the drenched landscape, telling myself it was unfair to feel critical of Boss—people just naturally wanted to be polite to other people's parents. But I also knew on that day that Boss and I would never get to be friends.

And in fact, in the end, the only real friends I made at the hospital I made at night. Possibly this was because there would only be two of us on a night ward, working seven to seven, and consequently we were overworked and so we would cheat. Up on the children's ward, which was raucous and huge and smelled of wet diapers and of all the sweet children's medicines for bronchitis and diarrhea, we would decide which of the dressings and treatments could most safely be skipped, and when four a.m. rolled around we wouldn't pick up the thermometer trays and go from room to room taking temperatures as we'd been instructed to do—instead, one of us would watch for the night supervisor while the other would sit at the night desk with a pen and a ruler and make a series of quick graphs from the temperatures we had invented a mere half-hour before. The desk, with the vaulted hospital darkness looming all around it—institutional, immense—would look like a desk on a stage set, and in the distance we would sometimes hear the elevators rising, then falling, our hearts in our throats until we heard them rise or fall past our floor. Sometimes the night supervisor would also surprise us by coming up the back stairs, although she never did manage to find us at our clandestine work on our graphs. But even without our fear of her, the night was a theatre to us and we were its actors, even months after we'd worked together we would hail each other, run into one another's arms, we had become (forever, it seemed) each other's own private little Night Family.

But day duty in the Nursery was the coveted stint, the one everyone wanted. On day duty in the Nursery we would give the babies their morning baths in sinks floored by wood slats, creaming their newborn bodies with liquid green soap from the hospital soap dispensers (punching the soap releasers so hard we'd sometimes jam them), then we'd hose down the green froth with warm water from hoses that could have been garden hoses. The new babies seemed huge to us, durable as rubber, especially compared to the babies in the Premature Nursery—tiny specimen-babies with lengths of clear tubing taped to their miniature nostrils.

It was only when we carried the full-term babies down the Maternity hallways and fitted them into the anxious arms of their mothers that they would let loose weak little newborn-baby cries, frail as wisps of smoke from the NO. (Which stood for Nurses Only and was the room where we smoked.) Here and there on Maternity there would also be a well-read young mother who would want her baby to have breast milk and so would hitch herself up in her bed to offer a shy nipple to her ravenous child. How cool and fragrant these new mothers' rooms were, potted jungles, but instead of a jungle stream sparkling by, there would be a small open-topped glass globe and at its bottom a dozen baby roses nestling in ice chips. I used to wonder what it would be like—to feel one of my breasts held with such dignified delicacy by such tiny hands.

But the big public surgery wards were another matter, and when Miss Poole demonstrated, for a small group of student nurses, the giving of an injection, I was terrified that my natural indecisiveness would make me a failure at it. Wasn't I always the last student to finish up my back rubs and Evening Care for the night? Other nurses couldn't help smiling, either, at the way I could never seem to get the right quantity of starch in my cap. Instead of standing up proudly, it was as limp as a hanky waved by a wilting woman leaving somewhere forever. But I also knew that I had a certain advantage over my classmates: I had been hospitalized for pneumonia while I was in high school and so had been in the perfect position to learn that the nurses and doctors who would lose their nerve as they approached the injection site were the ones who would bring certain pain to the patient. I could still recall the cool whiff of air each time my nightgown was shoved up by one of the interns or nurses, followed by the sensation that I was holding myself too tightly winced down there—that I was all secret sex thoughts and runaway heartbeat.

Miss Poole, meanwhile, was instructing us. On how to place a hand at the top curve of the hip. On how to draw a thumb halfway down the arc of an imaginary right angle. On how to press with the thumb as if pressing in a thumbtack. On how to fill the syringe and take aim.

We all took a turn. All took aim for the invisible bull's-eye, all plunged the needle into the tough (or soft) male skin of the eight men on Male Surgery who had offered themselves up as guinea pigs.

One of the guinea pigs even smiled up at Miss Poole. "Heroin?" he asked her.

"That'll be the day."

We all gazed at her, astounded. We had never thought of her as a woman who would flirt. Or be flirted with.

"What, then?" the guinea pig asked her.

"Sterile water."

"Aha. A placebo. Just what you cruel women give to all the bad little hypochondriacs. . . ."

Miss Poole smiled fleetingly down at him, and then even singled out three of the students for particular praise: "Miss Bostwick, Miss Gamble, Miss Bishop." The last of these names seemed to surprise her a great deal, she was so accustomed to my always being the last one to finish up my work for the night. As I was on my way off the ward she even gave me one of her small chilly bows. "Very *good*, Miss Bishop."

Back in the world of acronyms and medical jokes, the names of the doctors being paged over the P.A. made us want to invent better specialties for them: for Dr. Tingley (neurology); for Dr. Touchie (venereal diseases); for Dr. Plummer (urology); for Dr. Seymour (ophthalmology); for Dr. Rushforth (obstetrics).

Dr. Tannenbaum, my parents' GP in Wolfville, was not so appropriately named; at home the only nicknames we could manage to come up with for him were Herr Doktor and Dr. Christmas Tree. Not that I had many occasions to use either name. But I'd had to go to see him late one afternoon the summer I was seventeen and my sister Lorna was sixteen. Our mother drove the two of us downtown so that Lorna could pick up a pair of earrings at Zellers while I stopped off at Herr Doktor's to get a prescription for a bladder infection.

My mother had decided to come up to the second-floor clinic with me and sat leafing through a magazine while she waited for me to come out of the consultation room. And after Herr Doktor had examined me and was seeing me to the door of his office, she quickly got to her feet to call out, "Oh, Ben! Could I have just a very brief little word with you?"

The first thing I did after we got back home was swallow two tablets of sulfa with a glass of cold milk, but the cystitis was also making me feel oversexed and so I went up to my room to be alone for a while with my oversexed thoughts. I must have slept for a little bit too, because when I heard Lorna come running up the stairs I was confused for a moment and thought it was morning. But when she poked her head into my room it was only to tell me that she wanted to show me her new earrings. I groggily made my way into the bathroom to splash my face awake. While I was in there I also decided to soak one of my sweaters, and when I discovered that I had a stain on the front of my shirt I lifted one of the squeezed sweater sleeves up from the soapy water so that I could rub at the stain with it. It was at this point that Lorna (screwing in her new earrings) came into the bathroom to look at herself in the mirror over the sink.

She smiled at her reflection, then said, "Today I got almost as much attention as I needed to get."

Although I'd often resented and envied Lorna, and although she was our mother's little darling and I was not, this was one of the times I could really see it: why so many people thought she was an adorable girl. And how really admirable too, I thought, to be so honest about your own egomania.

She cupped the air just under her ears and bounced her earrings a little, turning her head in a pleased way to right and left. Then she looked down to see what I was doing. "God, that looks surreal. Like you're pawing at yourself with the hand of a person who's drowning."

I smiled, but I could feel her studying me at least as carefully as she'd studied her own earringed reflection.

"So," she said, after a long moment of scrutiny. "You're still a virgin."

I stared at our two faces in the mirror. "Who told you that?"

"Dr. Christmas Tree told Mother, and Mother told me."

Herr Doktor? How could that be? I was standing with a fist of wet sweater held pressed to a breast. I asked her what he had said. I couldn't imagine it.

"He said, 'You have no idea what a great *pleasure* it is, Mrs. Bishop, especially in this day and age, to discover that such a lovely young woman is still a *virgin*—'"

I wouldn't ever go back to see him again then. I would find myself another doctor. I wished I could also find myself another mother and sister. But what made me really angry when I thought of Mother gossiping about me to Lorna was the fact that I knew she had totally different standards for Lorna and me, and that if I got pregnant I'd be treated like an imbecile, a deranged slut, but if Lorna got pregnant she'd be flown off to visit an abortionist in some city like Buffalo and it would all be a lark. Of course certain facts must be faced, Mother and Lorna were pals and had been pals forever. Whereas Mother and I were only—what? We were Mother and Daughter. And then I remembered that Lorna, as a child, had liked to bite, and would bite my arm whenever we bickered. When no one was looking I would give her a brutal pinch back. But when one of the pinch marks filled up with a crescent of pus, I began to secretly minister to it with iodine and Ozonal. My interest in becoming a nurse dates from the summer of that medical intervention.

But it hurt me, to be dismissed as a virgin, when in earlier childhood I was sure that I'd been much more sex-obsessed than Lorna ever was. During the summers we were living at Cape Tormentine I had run wild with a whole crowd of cousins, and one of the girl cousins and I had slipped notes into the mailboxes of certain chosen older boy cousins with messages that said "Do you want to do you-know-what to us?" We had spied on older girl cousins too, while they were packing their luggage for schools whose names seemed to have come out of a fable—Netherwood, Edgehill, Horton Academy; we'd watched them pack sky blue hat boxes with new blue and grey sweaters, then watched them tear open new blue boxes of sanitary napkins and stuff dozens of these white napkins into the hat boxes to swim like white fishes in round blue and grey woollen seas. And we'd so relentlessly tormented a handsome older cousin named Jerry that he took to swatting at us with a wet towel. Which only made us feel so sexy that we pranced back and forth in front of him, little corporals of sex, our shoulders thrust back and our arms held very straight so that we could cup our stung bottoms while we taunted him, stepping our knees high.

The summer I turned eleven, Jerry made a pet out of a wounded crow that he'd found down on the beach and then he built a house for it out in the woods. It wasn't really a house, it was really a kind of free-standing cave made of spruce boughs with a dim interior that smelled of the sick smell of white bread soaked in milk. The crow would peck at the damp bread and then hobble about in front of his cave, flapping his wings and hoarsely calling out to his lost friends.

I began to go out there for visits, in love with Jerry while pretending to be in love with the crow. And it seems to me now that I was always wearing the same damp pink wool swimsuit that was a little too tight for me and a dry unbuttoned white blouse. The swimsuit's tightness and dampness felt very thrilling. Which suggests that I knew what I wanted. And I did. I wanted forbidden things to happen. To obey and disobey. If I'd had the vocabulary to describe my euphoria, I'd have had to say that during those sunlit afternoons I lived in a kind of depraved heaven. (Even though I always kept the swimsuit equivalent of my underpants on.) I also didn't know that there was a word for what I was feeling as Jerry and I rolled around on the floor of the forest—a word out there in the world of the innocent adults—but one evening when one of my older cousins was describing her reaction to a love scene in a movie by telling a roomful of her sisters "I nearly went through myself," I understood that she must have been feeling what I'd felt with Jerry.

But my happiness was short-lived; the following summer Jerry fell for an older girl who was an usherette at a movie house in Moncton and I was left in a state of aroused longing that felt as if it would never abate.

Up in the Case Room, the intern on the night shift was a Montrealer named Morris Cody, a med student from McGill. His nickname was Morse Code and he had the fixed gaze of someone who'd been sleep-deprived for weeks. Years, even. A bit after midnight, when I was down in the utility room stuffing bloody sheets into one of the wheeled hampers for laundry, he came in to ask me if I could come with him for a minute or two. "I've got a possible eclampsia in thirty-six and I'm going to be needing your help."

I followed him quickly down the dim nighttime hallway with its maroon plastic vases of flowers standing like sentries to the right and left of each door, and as I hurried behind him I kept nervously trying to review what I knew about eclampsia. The word made me think of a dangerous dampness—or was I only thinking of the word "damp" because it rhymed with the "clamp" of eclampsia? And no detectable heartbeat. But no, that couldn't be right.

According to her chart, the eclampsia patient was nineteen. My age, exactly, but she reminded me more of Lorna. Heavy and creamy, she even had Lorna's short-cropped sleek hair.

Code shoved up the back of the patient's hospital gown, exposing the creamy Lorna-like buttocks, then told me to give her a shot of Demerol. "I think we're going to have to prepare her for a C-section." And after I'd given her the injection he even smiled at me with a sleepy radiance that seemed almost sexual. "Hey, you're a pro." Then he told me to keep on monitoring her blood pressure while he ran over to the OR to book her for surgery.

I felt honoured to have been left in charge of this dangerously ill and young pregnant person, and between taking readings of her blood pressure I massaged her nearest shoulder. I always felt a little extra alert when I had to look after a patient who was the same age as I was. I would have felt the same way if someone my own age had died. Would have wanted to stop total strangers on the street to say to them: "Do you know what's just happened? Someone who's exactly the same age as I am has just died, can you believe it?"

But waiting for Code to come back, I was only thinking of how much I disliked the word "buttocks." So cold and clinical. But at the same time so pig-like. Like pork hocks. And then I named to myself all the synonyms for buttocks and buttock. Ass was too loose and had too much jounce in it to be used for anyone but a woman, and the same went for derrière. And backside and behind and bottom were what adults used for children. And bum was what *children* used for children. I thought of my mother's buttocks in their silky tan slacks and of how, when I was five or six, I used to come up behind her and give her a hug and rest my cheek against one of them. "Cheek to cheek," Lorna would probably have said if I'd told her about it, but I must still have loved our mother back then because I could still remember how much I used to love to watch her getting dressed and undressed, I even used to daydream about her clothes, which ones I wanted her to wear, which ones I thought she was most pretty in. She had a clutch purse that looked like a giant zippered envelope made out of a mosaic of red and white plastic chiclets and she had a hat called a sissy sailor, a tilted half-veiled buckram hat that had navy blue velvet dots on its short navy blue veil, the dots the size of the pupil in an eye. She was like one of the more gorgeous of the older girls at school, one of the ones the littler girls fawned over at recess. The one whose affection I most longed to win.

Code came back, followed by two orderlies with a stretcher. "How's the patient?"

"She's stayed stable."

"Good stuff."

Another year passed. Then Boss and I were both briefly on night shift (although on different wards) the following December, and the night of the Christmas dance we ran over to the residence for a stolen five minutes to watch our classmates dancing. We hurried up the main stone steps and then stood in the arched doorway to the lounge with our nurses' capes hugged around us while we tried to get a glimpse of everyone's boyfriends and dresses.

In an anteroom off the lounge, two senior students and one of the night supervisors were sitting smoking. They glanced at us briefly, striking terror in our younger hearts, even though they did not look at us unkindly, only with an abstracted social interest, as if their minds were entirely on the dance and the dancers.

And then it was Christmas. I was to have Christmas Day off. Boss was going to go home for Christmas Day too, but instead of packing, she was sitting slumped on her bed with her nubby dark winter coat pulled on over her uniform because the radiator in our room was kaput.

"I've got something to show you," she said, and I saw that her hands, under her bib, were working to unpin something. Then one hand backed its way out from beneath her pinafore, holding a safety pin, and hanging from the safety pin there was a ring. It was an engagement ring with nine tiny diamonds circling a diamond the size of a thumbtack. It was the most spectacular diamond ring I had ever seen, but Boss said that the man she was marrying was not really all that terribly rich. "He only owns one little gas station." I had to repress a small smile—wasn't owning one little gas station quite rich enough? But she was looking really quite sad, I thought, sitting with such shy weariness on her bed in her heavy dark coat.

Lorna had decided to stay in Halifax and spend Christmas with friends of hers from Dal, and because of her absence, the polished house with only our parents in it seemed to announce with every heartbeat that life was elsewhere. "But isn't it wonderful?" cried my mother. "That she has so many friends?"

I went up to my room to lie down on my bed, but I was feeling too restless to rest. I went to my window to look out over the town. I think I was looking for my former future, the future I had dreamed of when I was in grade school—the astounding future I would have when I got to be nineteen.

As for the weather, it had been a clear night when I'd come into Wolfville on the bus, but a snow squall blew up just as my parents were setting off to do last-minute shopping for candles and wine. After I heard the car back out of the garage, I made a visit to Lorna's room. Snow hissed at her windows as I opened her closet door and looked in at her shoes. Also at her evening gowns—a drop-waisted mauve taffeta with capped taffeta sleeves; a dance dress with a strapless black velvet bodice and a filmy layer of black chiffon over a straight pink taffeta skirt. I slipped my feet into a pair of bruised silver sandals that looked as if they had been worn by a giantess with bunions, then tried on the strapless black velvet. It was so loose that I had to squeeze a fistful of its soft bodice tight behind me while I breathed in its smell of perspiration and dancing. I vamped at myself in the mirror and tried to imagine not being a student nurse any more. Going to college. What terrified me most about being at the hospital was the fear that I would kill someone. I was in the habit of daydreaming, thinking of other things, and when I was pouring out cough syrups or counting out capsules, I would often forget, after recapping, to recheck the labels on vials and bottles and this would occasionally lead to my sitting wildly up in my bed in the middle of the night, convinced that I had given someone someone else's pills or injection.

I went to church with my parents on Christmas morning. It was a cold clear day with winter sunlight pouring in through the purple robes of the saints in the stained-glass windows. There was a stained-glass window at the hospital too, in the lab on the ground floor of the nurses' residence, and a purple-robed saint gazed down on a congregation there as well. But on Tuesdays and Thursdays the congregation the saint looked down on was made up of two rows of young women with knives. It was also under this stained-glass window—the lab had once been the old wing's library—that I'd got my first sight of the skinned rats we had to dissect for anatomy lab. White as ivory, as bone, they were suspended in formaldehyde in big clear glass Mason jars, a rat to a bottle—embryonic, humanoid, half-rat, half-baby—and as my parents and I joined the church's congregation in shouting out "Joy to the World!" I watched the two dark-coated old Anglicans who were making their way up and down the aisles with the brass collection plates—they were both completely bald and one of them quite eerily resembled one of the bottled rats—and I couldn't help but recall the pulsing live spots of churchy light that had been sent to skitter across the wall by the laboratory door, spots of light made by the wind raking its sun spots across that part of the window where the saint's limp white duck feet were suspended in a lead-bordered band of blue glass.

But just before the end of the service there was a small cry down at the back, and at once we were all on our feet and craning back to see. It was one of the old men who had passed around the plates for the money—he had fallen in a dark heap to the carpet. By the time we got back to him, a bald man in a duffle coat was kneeling beside him, undoing the buttons on his shirt, loosening his tie. I was incredibly relieved that this kneeling person (doctor? fireman?) was among us, and it was then that I realized I'd been feeling almost faint from the fear that as possibly the only medical person present, some life-saving action would be required of me and I wouldn't at all know what to do.

On our way out of the church we bumped into Jerry who told us that his parents had gone off to Florida for Christmas.

"But then you must come and have dinner with us," said my mother.

My heart sank as Jerry said yes, even though he said yes with the air of one who would rather say no but didn't quite dare to say no. In his navy overcoat and pressed grey flannels, his hair standing up with rooster primness in the cold, he walked beside me in silence across the new snow to our car, then climbed into the back seat to sit on my right. We hadn't said one single word to one another, and it seems to me now that if a man with a gun had at that moment given us an order—*Speak, or I will be forced to shoot you both dead*—we would have been in danger of deciding we had no choice but to be shot.

My mother, meanwhile, was eager to speculate on the fate of the fallen Anglican.

"Probably nothing serious at all!" I called heartlessly out from my perch on the back seat. "Poor old guy probably forgot to eat breakfast before he ran over to the church this morning."

At this she turned to accuse me of having become terribly hard-hearted. "And you used to be such a sweet girl," she told me.

I looked out the window. It embarrassed me extremely to have such a thing said to me in front of Jerry. I thought (and the diction of my thought struck me as being the embittered diction of a Victorian governess): "So this is how I am informed of my virtues—by being told that I no longer possess them." But I didn't answer my mother; I only watched Wolfville's snowed-in gardens and driveways float depressingly by. "Don't turn your back on the sick," my mother had said to me one Sunday morning last summer, just after I'd told her that I couldn't see what was all that superb about modern medicine. But then my mother loved hospitals, loved doctors, thought all doctors were gods. "Lots of people leave that hospital a whole lot sicker than they were the day they came into it," I'd told her in my new adult voice, a voice that said "I've seen people die." And I had in fact seen seven people die by that time. I had even seen a three-year-old child die. But the three-year-old child who'd died was not the child I was remembering now—the child I was remembering now was a newborn baby boy whose parents had arranged to have him circumcised in one of the anterooms off the Maternity Ward. Just after the surgery, they'd invited me to come in and drink a celebratory glass of brandy with them. There was a treat for the baby as well: a sugar cube wrapped up in gauze that had been soaked in a capful of the same brandy. Between wails, he took violent and gobbling sucks at it. The parents were Jewish parents in a Protestant part of the country—the father, who was scholarly but hairy, was even wearing a white satin skullcap that he had drawn out of his briefcase—and I felt honoured to have been invited to eat one of the flat Jewish cookies, to sip from the small glass of (possibly Jewish) brandy, to be the one student the parents had decided would be tolerant enough to be invited to a Jewish celebration. I admired the wife as well—she was so tiny and warm-eyed and perfumed and quick. But at the same time that I was being offered the cookies and brandy, I couldn't help but feel pity for the baby. Not that I hadn't seen circumcised baby penises before—but only in colour plates in a medical textbook. But this was the real thing; this was serene butchery—festive and ancient. And the following week there was even a postscript: one of the doctors who lectured to us on anatomy and physiology told us that because Jewish men were circumcised, Jewish women had incredibly low rates of cancer of the cervix. "Unless, of course, they marry guys who are goys."

The candles' flames were pale in the glare of the noontime winter sunlight, and for some reason this phantom candlelight in sunlight was making me feel very tense. But Jerry's presence directly across from me was making me feel very tense too, and while I was eating my turkey I found myself trying not to think of our summer afternoons out in the woods and then I tried not to think of the lab in the nurses' residence and the way that the lab end of the hallway always smelled of formaldehyde and rat flesh. But then I began to be afraid that I'd convince myself that the turkey meat was rat meat and that I'd have to get up from the table and be sick. And so it seemed to me that it was to take my mind off both Jerry and the bottled rats that I said in a voice whose invented calm made my heart gallop, "I've been thinking of leaving training."

"No!" cried my mother. And then she said, "But you've been so happy there."

I thought of the books I had read during my two years at the hospital—nothing but medical textbooks filled with greyish photos of white rats and pictures of skinny men in too-large black gym shorts who were suffering from curvature of the spine or ringworm.

As for Jerry, he didn't look up at me, but I could tell from the way he'd stopped chewing that he was giving the conversation his attention.

I said in a low voice, almost a whisper, "I wouldn't say *happy*. . . ."

"But you used to write Daddy and me such happy happy letters. That time you were on that ward with all those men. . . ."

My father laughed. And even Jerry smiled a little, although he didn't look up.

"And you've been such wonderful friends with that darling girl you brought home with you—"

"Holly," said my father, surprising me.

My mother spoke in her most innocent voice: "Is *she* leaving?" I refused to answer. I knew she knew she was not.

"Such a charmer," said my mother in the offensively dreamy voice she sometimes used when she was about to praise Lorna. "And real character and endurance too."

I found myself wanting to answer her in a completely opposite sort of voice, in a private fierce voice, found myself wanting to say to her, "Holly is wild, Mother. She's wilder than anybody." I even found myself wanting to tell her that Holly had syphilis and had been accepted as a candidate for the nursing school only because her father had worn his cleric's collar when he'd gone to sweet-talk the superintendent into letting her in. But how could I do that? When Boss had sat looking so weary and womanly on the side of her bed while she'd told me she would marry? And in any case, wild was the very last word anyone who knew her would have used to describe her. I said, "You hardly even know her, for heaven's sake. She was only here for one afternoon."

Jerry looked up at this, looked directly at me.

But then lunch was over and it was time for him to be off.

My mother and I stood and watched him walk down the front path to the street.

"A really awfully nice young man," said my mother.

Yes.

And then the daylight was going and it was time for me to go too. My mother sprayed herself with Tabu just before she pulled on her coat, and the powerful scent of it perfumed the cold vinyl smell of the air inside the car. All the way to the station I had only one prayer: Please please dear God, let her not praise Lorna.

It was a relief, at the train chalet, to step out into the freezing and clear Fundy night. Only the crunch of snow underfoot and a calm shine on the ocean.

At the foot of the steps to the last passenger car, my mother gave me a hard hug meant to inject me with character, with spirit. "Courage, darling," she said, pronouncing "courage" affectedly, in the French manner. "That's all it's going to take, just a little more courage and stick-to-it-ness."

All the way back home on the train—for the hospital was, in its way, home to me now—I composed an imaginary letter to my mother, a letter she would never be able to say was a happy happy letter, a letter that examined the difference between courage and endurance. You think they are the same thing, I imagined writing, but they are not; in this case they are opposites. But what did I want then, if I didn't want to stay at the hospital? You could not turn your back on the sick, not unless you had some other plan. And then I remembered how I had wanted, when I had first started training, to be connected, in some useful way, to emergency, heroic acts. And if I hadn't actually wanted to marry a doctor, I had certainly hoped to find (and be attractive to) the sort of man who would have the quality that the most heroic of the doctors seemed to have: an ill-tempered calm in the face of emergency that suggested a passionate nature. I suppose I had hoped it would be contagious—a good contagion—and that I too would become a calm person who could act fast and know what was what.

But now I only sat on the train and made two lists for myself. What I hated about the hospital, what I loved. What I hated: never getting enough sleep, and being constantly terrified that I'd make a mistake dispensing the pills and giving injections. I also hated wiping non-existent dust from stainless-steel shelves with liquid ether. And why had we been ordered to dust what was dustless? Because it was a make-work sort of work, work we were told to do because those madwomen supervisors could not bear to see young women idle. The ether was freezing too, it burned our fingertips with a cold that felt as deep and eternal as the cold of dry ice—cold with an afterlife—and its sedative vapours made me feel sick and woozy.

And on the good list I put watching babies being born and above all watching their hot little heads pushing wide the shaved pods of flesh between their mother's raised thighs, and then I listed everything else about the Case Room that I loved—feeding the babies, and hosing them down with rubber hoses for their morning baths and then wrapping them up as tight as cigars to be carried out into a world of waiting arms and flowers. And for the surgery wards I listed giving injections and ballooning up the rubber gloves and then punching the captured air until it popped, in sequential squirts, into fat rubber fingers.

The train conductor came to collect the tickets a little after ten. He made me think of the first dead patient I had seen. The dead man had been overweight and in his forties, freckled and sour-smelling. He had seemed too sour and freckled, really, to be dead. He had looked like a Sunday athlete. When I had at last been able to make myself stop trembling from touching the body of someone who was truly dead, I had imagined the body's owner alive, a football lightly held to make teasing dips back and forth in the air just in front of the genitals, the footwork taunting and fancy, the eyes alive with dreams of athletic dives and escapes.

Was it possible that this train conductor was the dead man's brother? He punched my ticket quite athletically, I thought, before handing it back to me. After he had gone off, I looked out the window at the part of the sky where the most stars seemed to have been flung and remembered the scatter of spike-heeled shoes on the floor of Lorna's closet, then remembered that once, years ago, when I'd dropped the ball during a neighbourhood baseball game, Lorna had screeched "Dummie!" at me. I knew that when I left the hospital I would just have to do it and not ask for anyone's permission. I tried to think of my leaving as playing a game of darts and picking up a dart with a syringe attached to it and taking perfect aim for a buttock.

A MAD MAZE MADE BY
GOD

TINKLE NEARBY.

Bracelet?

They drew themselves clumsily up.

It was Mitzi, standing in the living-room doorway and aiming her gaze at the wall above the couch where they'd been lying as if she'd decided that the polite thing to do would be to pretend not to see them. But Barbara couldn't help feeling that if they were both people the child was pretending not to see, then she was the person she was pretending not to see most.

"Dad?" said Mitzi. "Isn't it time for us to go home soon? I have homework and stuff."

And Bruce clearly felt so fallen, was so much the fallen gentleman, that he hitched up the belt on his jeans and immediately stumbled up and said yes.

Bruce's first wife, Rosalie, killed herself. Two years before Bruce and Barbara first met. What Barbara knew about Bruce's wife was that she had been moody and beautiful. And she knew Rosalie was beautiful because not long after she'd been introduced to Bruce he had shown her a photo. In it, an unsmiling and spectacular young woman in a pair of wrinkled white shorts and a sleeveless black T-shirt was standing in an arched, sunlit doorway. Shoulder-length straight fair hair, sun-whitened on top, framed a face that was innately lively, even if it was a liveliness darkened by a thoughtful depression. Barbara was ashamed of the rush of jealous awe she had felt. How could anyone that beautiful want to kill herself? The eyes were so limpid. And although it was inaccurate, the word limpid also occurred to her in connection with one of the drooping white hands. A hand that at a younger age might have trailed a doll by the foot. Or, in another century, a rose by its stem end, but which in the photograph trailed an unlit cigarette.

But according to Bruce, Rosalie was not vain. "She was too busy keeping track of her grudges to have any time left over for vanity. Besides, she took her good looks for granted. She was used to them, she'd always had them. I'm not even sure she approved all that much of physical beauty. She was a very pure, very puritanical sort of person."

After deciding not to ask what she most wanted to ask, Barbara asked it: "Why did you marry her?"

A finger outlined one of her eyes, her mouth. (They were lying on her couch again.) "I thought she was the most beautiful woman I had ever laid eyes on. I was also terrified of her. Life with her was just one big surprise after another."

Barbara did not consider herself to be the beautiful type, and she was certainly not the terrifying type either—she was a small and plump voluptuous blonde who looked as if she didn't have a care in the world. Which was also one of the world's great jokes because she was a worrier. A worrier and also a depressed person herself. Right now, for instance: the way Bruce's finger was outlining her eye, then her mouth, was making her feel so sad she was afraid her eyes would start to well up. The finger seemed to her to be feeling quite sad as well, seemed to remember happier days spent tracking another eye, other lips. She whispered, "Und so. You found that arousing, Herr Dwyer? Being terrified?"

"Maybe," said Bruce, pulling her on top of him.

Half laughing, she dipped down to him to hide her face against his shoulder. She didn't want him looking so trustingly up into her eyes when she didn't even know what message he'd be able to read in them. One message he might read was that she was now imagining a scene in which he was kissing her. And to her "Do you want to make love?" he was hoarsely whispering, "Terrify me." In reality she was just barely repressing the desire to say, "What if you're the sort of man whose wives all do themselves in, one after another?" But it was insane to think that, he was only unlucky. She was still feeling a bit down, though, and was afraid she might start to cry for no reason. She imagined dripping tears onto his face, or lying beside him and so copiously weeping that she'd end up with tears in her ears and tears in her hair and tears dampening the armpit of his shirt till it would get soaking wet.

It snowed during the wedding ceremony, which took place in the almost unfurnished, tall-windowed living room of some friends of

Bruce's, in a newly remodelled old stone house overlooking Strathcona Park. There was only one painting in the room, the fur flank of some animal too mammoth even for that giant canvas. A huge gash ran like a red path down a field of grey fur, but halfway across the field the fur turned into a black bog with a beaded corroded purple festering at its industrial eastern edge.

Bruce's best man was his cousin Steve, and Barbara's attendant was her best friend Connie, a willowy woman with a whimsical judging smile who had tucked a silk shirt into a long skirt the dead impenetrable blue of a schoolgirl's gym tunic. Two nights before the wedding, when Connie and Barbara were working together out in Barbara's kitchen, taking turns squirting pink frosting piping all over the wedding cake, Connie had started clowning around with the veil Barbara had brought home from a bride shop. It was too white for Barbara's dress and so they'd finally decided to steep it in a pot of hot tea. It had turned out stunningly well—a classy diaphanous fawn—and was now the perfect thing for the creamy eyelet dress Barbara was wearing instead of a wedding gown.

Just as the reception was about to begin, the wedding party was summoned out to the front steps of the house to be posed between two stone urns by the photographer. It was snowing, the thick, slow snow of a mild March day, and Bruce caped his jacket over Barbara's shoulders. The next-door neighbours returned from a ski trip in the middle of the photo-taking. They were a laughing group of men and women in their early twenties and when they saw that there'd been a wedding they came over to offer congratulations. Then one of the women came up with the idea of making a wedding arch for the bride and groom, and so several of the photographs later showed Barbara and Bruce laughingly ducking their way in under an archway of ski poles—

the closest they came that day to being in anything even faintly resembling a church—and looking bashfully jubilant. (Which was not how Barbara could recall having felt at the time.)

Because after the photos, there was the high anxiety of the reception. Not anxiety about Tim, clearly in his element as the son of one of the principal performers, but about Mitzi. She seemed to be making a point of looking so utterly unimpressed, her small face fierce above its tight nosegay of flowers. Possibly she was in a rage about the outfit she was wearing, picked out at the last minute by Bruce's mother. It was certainly true that there was something too foolishly and commercially ethnic about it, with its crude green embroidery bordering the edges of a red felt bolero, and its shiny black skirt and silk knee-socks.

And then out in the kitchen, a man Barbara had never seen before saluted her with an olive. "The bride!"

But it seemed to Barbara that his voice was maliciously effusive; gazing at her with drunken seriousness from above a necktie that looked as if it had been woven out of bits of bright straw he called out "Congratulations!" to her, and then told her (twice) that she was one lucky lady.

She spoke to him in a small cold voice, out of fear. "Are you a friend of Bruce's?"

He seemed to want her to think he found her question diverting. "Old friends," he said.

Had he put a certain stress on the "old"? Barbara thought so. And after she had loaded up her tray with fresh drinks, she went back to the living room, wanting to find Bruce. But he was occupied—dancing with Arlene, a nurse from Steve's clinic. And so after she'd handed around the drinks she was left with nothing to do but pretend to be hungry at the buffet table that Bruce had shoved over to the west wall to get the best of the light from the three big bay windows. Bruce's mother was over there too, laying strips of smoked salmon down on slices of rye. Her pale pink linen suit looked as if it had been beaded by droplets of ice, and her pale quick eyes seemed to be filling up with sums: additions, detractions. "Lovely and informal and sweet" was what she said now, smiling with social vagueness out at the dancers. Was this a critical comment, meant to indicate that the wedding was too casual? It *was* casual (by design!) but Barbara, piling potato salad onto a small flowered plate while trying to pretend she wasn't watching Bruce and Arlene, only absently said yes in what she feared must be a very cracked and dry voice. When the tape ended, she watched Bruce walk Arlene over to talk with Connie. She hoped (and also believed) that he was looking more polite than entranced. Then she saw him gaze around the room, looking for her. But as he was making his way over to her he got waylaid by some of the other guests. She watched him talking to Steve and to an old editor friend of hers, and something about the way he was smiling made her recall that when she'd first described him to Connie she'd said, "I've met this new person. A mechanical engineer. Which makes him sound dull, but he's really not. He's into solar energy and he travels all over the country spreading the solar gospel." And then when Connie had asked her to describe his looks she'd said that he looked like a blacksmith but dressed like a scoutmaster—khaki shirts and Bermudas, canvas jackets. But on this day, his wedding day, he was a blacksmith in a black business suit.

When he came over to Barbara they embraced lightly and then she kept her arm around his waist and walked him, with a few jokey dance steps, out of earshot of his mother. His midriff seemed consoling to her, seemed to beam out an overweight and affectionate heat. But she was still feeling a little too thin-skinned and bridal and so couldn't keep herself from saying, "Remember me? I'm the girl you married."

He started to dance her out into the middle of the room. "You still love me, I hope."

"Who is Malcolm?"

"Malcolm?" He seemed puzzled. But then he remembered. "Oh, Malcolm," he said. "He's a client. He gave us so much work last year he saved us from going under. Why? Is he here?" He looked back over his shoulder. "I don't see him."

"He's out in the kitchen."

"What happened? Did he say some horrible Malcolm-like thing to you?"

"He tried to give me the impression that you two have some sort of sexual history."

Bruce listened, eyes narrowed, wondering. But then he only said, "He's just jealous of you, sweetheart. Probably he wants to be the bride himself. Just think of him as the bad fairy at our wedding."

Barbara knew it was childish of her to feel spooked by having prophetic-seeming remarks made to her on her wedding day, but the bad-fairy remark reminded her of something her ex-husband's father had said to her the night before her marriage to Eduardo. In Montreal, this was, nearly thirteen years ago. "Playing second fiddle, I see," he'd said to her, smiling at her with a look that had seemed to her to be both condemning and flirtatious. She'd tried to tell herself that he didn't really mean anything bad by it—he was at that time still a recent immigrant to Canada and occasionally used idioms oddly. Probably he'd only said it because she'd set a plate of biscuits down on a tacky ornamental table shaped like a fiddle. And yet the remark had been prophetic: Eddie, a journalist whose beat was Queen's Park, had turned out to be a heartbreaker.

After the wedding, Bruce sold the house in which Rosalie had killed herself and he and Mitzi moved in with Barbara and Tim. Barbara was renting a two-bedroom apartment in a row house in downtown Ottawa—in Sandy Hill—so there wasn't a great deal of space, but it only had to do them until October when the house Bruce was building for them was due to be finished.

Tim's admiration for his new stepsister made him kind. He gave up his bedroom for her and moved down to a cot in a plywood-panelled room in the basement. And Bruce and Barbara were able to compromise reasonably well on their two different approaches to child-rearing. (Bruce was strict, Barbara was not.)

Still, Bruce's parental certitudes and hearty good health depressed Barbara a little, and one evening in late April when Bruce had taken Tim for a swim at their neighbourhood pool and Barbara and Connie were alone in the house, drinking glasses of wine and making raisin bread, Barbara said, "Sometimes he's just so hard on the kids, sometimes he just isn't fair to them. He can be so brusque. Earlier today, for instance. . . ." And then she started to tell Connie about how Mitzi had begged to be allowed to go to a summer camp that five or six of her girlfriends were going to. "I know we could afford it because it's only for one tiny little week, but Bruce told her no, not this summer, maybe next year when we've partly paid for the house." She had tried to cheer Mit up by telling her how much she herself had despised being sent to camp when she was a child. But Mit had not been consoled. And then Tim had appeared in the doorway to stand beside his new sister. "I wouldn't go to camp if you paid me," he'd said.

By now the two women were both kneading and punching

the dough for the bread. (Sipping wine and punching.) It must have been the breastiness of the dough that had made Barbara think of camp in the first place, because what had been particularly awful about camp was the laughter of her tent-mates when they'd caught her carrying out a little breast-growing ritual that she'd pioneered. The only girl in the whole world to think of such a thing. Or so she'd thought then. "I had this little—procedure," she said to Connie, and she cupped her floury hands up under her breasts, turning the front of her black T-shirt cloudy. "I would sit up on the side of my bed in my pyjama bottoms and I'd go like this three times every night, and then I would whisper, 'Grow, grow, grow. . . . '"

Connie stood listening, half smiling, her wineglass pressed high up against a flushed cheek.

"I only did it when I was alone in the tent, but one night I forgot."

Connie said she'd never had a yen to go to her local girls' camp, a collection of whitewashed old huts on a muddy river. "I refused to. I was convinced it would be a fascist place with saluting the flag and bed-making inspection."

Barbara said the worst day was Sunday. "My parents could never get to see me. But they would always promise to come. On Sunday mornings there'd always be a long distance call for me and I'd have to go up to the main lodge, and it would be my mother saying, 'Darling, we're so sorry, but we won't be able to make it, after all—unexpected company has just dropped by.' And then all the company would come on the phone and talk to me too. Strange men, or at least men I didn't remember ever meeting before, would shout at me, 'How's my girl?' and strange women would say, 'Honey, I hope you are learning to swim.' Afterwards I would go and hide down by the outhouses so that no one would know that my parents hadn't come. And guess where the outhouses were." She set her wineglass down on the counter and folded her arms tight up under her breasts. "Guess."

"Oh hell, I don't know. Down by the kitchen."

"Don't make me puke," said Mitzi.

The two women turned to her, startled. How long have *you* been here, their two sets of eyes asked her. In the *house?*

"Okay," said Connie. "Okay. Not the kitchen." She sat down to think. "How about the archery field? You were lurking among the trees behind the archery field, angling to get yourself shot."

Mitzi poured herself a glass of cranberry juice. "What would she want to do that for?" she whispered, and Barbara felt a little afraid for her. This kind of talk might frighten her, make her think of her mother. But Connie was a bit drunk and seemed to want to keep on the topic. "Like those poor desperate soldiers," she said. "The ones who shoot themselves in the foot."

Mitzi sat down at the kitchen table and stared at the raisin dough as if mesmerized by it. "Why would they want to do that?"

"So they won't have to fight."

"Oh."

After Mitzi had left, it took a while for the two women to begin talking again. Finally Barbara said in a low voice, "You don't think she heard us talking, do you? About Bruce?"

Connie shook her head vehemently. A friend's no.

Barbara went to the bottom of the stairs and called up. "Mit? Are you up there?"

There was a sea sound—an upstairs surf in the trees.

"Mitzi?"

But she must have gone out again.

On a morning three months after the bread-making evening, Tim was down in his basement bedroom, packing his knapsack for wilderness camp. The camp was on Lake Temagami, north of North Bay. (He had changed his mind about camp by this time—he and Mitzi had taken over each other's positions and Tim was now keen to go because a friend had talked him into being his cabin-mate, and Mitzi had turned against the idea of camp absolutely and wanted to stay at home and be with her friends in the city.)

Tim's cabin-mate was to be Michael, his best friend from school. But on the morning that Tim and Michael were to be driven to the camp by Bruce, Michael's mother phoned to say that Michael had developed a fever and wouldn't be able to go after all.

Barbara went down to Tim's room to tell him. But her heart broke for him as she came down the stairs, he seemed so little and pale, crouched on his cot like a worried white lizard, taking in the bad news; Michael was the only person he knew who was planning to go. Barbara sat down beside him. "If you don't want to go, you don't have to," she told him. "Really. Only go if you really want to."

"But if I don't go, won't you lose your deposit?"

She said she didn't give a damn about the deposit. "Don't think about the money. Just do what you want to do." She considered saying more. She considered saying, "Sometimes the brave thing in life is to be willing to look like a coward," but the thought of how horrified Bruce would be if he ever got wind of her having said it made her hold her tongue.

There was a noise upstairs. Back door being unlatched, then heavy boots coming into the kitchen and walking across the floor directly over their heads. They could hear the door to the basement stairs creak open, and then Bruce's voice calling down, magnified, hollowly cheerful: "Ready, Tim?"

Tim stared at his pile of gear on the floor. "I'll be up in a minute!"

"Wait here a moment," Barbara whispered to him, and she climbed the stairs to the kitchen.

"Bruce!" she called in a warning whisper, although he was practically standing right beside her, drinking a glass of pineapple juice. She held him by his free wrist and drew him into the dining room, told him the story of the phone call from Michael's mother. "And I'm pretty sure Tim is having second thoughts too. So let's not put him under any pressure to go, okay?"

"Now you quit this," Bruce whispered fiercely back. "You've always babied this boy and now you're trying to baby him again."

But they had to stop, Tim was coming up the stairs with his stuff.

They came out to the kitchen to meet him.

"Great, Tim. You go load your gear into the car and I'll get the food for our lunch from your mum."

Tim edged by them, his knapsack on his back, his sleeping-roll hugged tightly to him. To Barbara he looked as drained and white as a boy going off to the wars. She said, "Wait a sec, hon," and she adjusted the front buckles on the straps of his knapsack, then brushed his hair back from his forehead and gave him a quick kiss near his hairline. "I put in some envelopes so you can write to us. And we'll write to you too. We'll write every day."

"We'll write every ten minutes," said Bruce, making Tim smile.

Barbara said she'd be sending him a parcel of cookies on the weekend. "And you can phone us any time at all, if you want to talk."

"But, Mum—it's a wilderness camp."

They all laughed at that.

Barbara stood in the doorway and watched them walk out to the street. She had decided not to go out to the car to say goodbye, she was too afraid she'd set Tim off crying. Bruce was loping along in his jeans and a white nylon windbreaker. Tim, beside him, was carrying his shoulders too stiff and too straight. At the car he turned to wave to her. Bruce waved to her too, but his wave was instructively brisk. She stood in the doorway and waved until they were out of her sight.

After they'd gone, she ran down to the basement apple barrel to get herself an apple. Eating it, she felt as if she'd been holding her breath ever since the night of Tim's birth. She couldn't imagine she'd ever get to feel the same way about Mit. She went up to the kitchen to make herself tea and then switched on the radio. But the announcer, like an announcer in a bad dream, was talking about a child who'd been camping with his family in the bush north of Temagami. The child was five years old and had wandered away from the campsite two nights before. Alistair, his name was. His parents had formed a search party and had spent two nights and a day desperately trying to find him.

How dangerous the country was! And how ready and willing life always was to dovetail bad news to the fear of the moment. Barbara thought of Tim, and in order to stop thinking of him, thought of Mit. Safely off at the pool with a crowd of her friends. A safe city child. At least so long as she kept her wits about her.

After Mitzi had come home for lunch, and then was off again, Barbara again turned on the news. By now fresh small-shoed tracks had been discovered in the sand near a stream. "So little Alistair is still walking around," said the announcer. And then he quoted the highest temperature for the day in that part of the north country and it was terribly hot, as the north always was hot in the summer, much hotter than it was farther south. Barbara looked out the window, taking tiny neat sips of her tea. Mitzi was back again, standing out on the sidewalk with a friend named Melanie, talking to two boys Barbara had never noticed before. Mit was so deeply tanned that she was by now a very brown girl, in fact a brown girl all over—brown eyes, blunt-cut shining brown hair hanging straight to her shoulders, brown sandals, brown shorts buttoned over her faded and puckered swimsuit. The part of the suit that showed above the shorts made Barbara think of chocolate rosebuds, but the swimsuit's puckers were a faded pink, not faded chocolate. And it seemed to her that Mit was still a child in the way that she stood, staring at the boys she was talking to with a frank, intelligent watchfulness. But Melanie was a creamy and conniving girl, white-skinned and black-haired and in a skimpy black bikini with nothing on over it but a short flowered voile hostess coat that she'd probably borrowed from her mother. There was something puffy and prematurely middle-aged about her, a kind of sexual staleness that made Barbara grateful that she was not the girl who was her new daughter.

Even in the city, the heat was intense. It kept affecting Barbara's concentration. She was supposed to be editing a report for one of her contacts at Secretary of State. She sat with the report at the dining-room table and made little marks on it. At ten to four she went upstairs to go to the bathroom and then detoured into

Bruce's and her bedroom to lie down on their bed. She took off her blouse and lay down on her back in nothing but her skirt. Her hair felt oiled; even her breasts felt oiled, they were so slippery with sweat. She didn't plan to sleep, sleeping in the daytime always made her feel drugged, worthless, she only wanted to lie near the fan for a bit and not think. But then she started to feel sexy. It was her nipples, they were feeling shrunken and aroused by the cool breeze from the fan. She tilted her hips and placed her hand on herself as if she were about to take the oath of allegiance, but too far down on her body. For some reason this made her think of the expression, They vote with their feet. But she couldn't do anything at all to relieve her condition, it would only compound the feeling of worthlessness. She also didn't have the energy for it. But there was also another reason: ever since Tim had been old enough to be away from home now and then, she hadn't been able to make love to herself when he was out in the world and exposed to its dangers. It was as if her own pleasure put his safety at risk and so she had to concentrate on protecting him always when he was out of her sight. She'd only been able to do it when he was at home and had his door closed and was in his own bed and asleep.

And now that he was up in the bush he'd be requiring her protection more than ever. She also had Bruce's safety to think of. And she thought again of the little lost boy, listlessly wandering in the hot endless forest. She and Eduardo had lost Tim once, the summer he was the same age as Alistair. They'd been visiting a pavilion at the Canadian National Exhibition, and Tim had had to go to the bathroom. Eduardo said he would take him, but a few minutes after they'd gone off, Barbara glanced up to see Eduardo making his frantic way back to her. "He was right behind me! But then I turned around and he was gone!"

They had pushed back through the crowd like crazed people, over to the toilets, away from the toilets, back the way they had come, off to the left, up the stairs, down. At last they'd run back toward the main entrance, toward the haunted bright light of a cold September day, threading their way breathlessly among the moronically unconcerned people streaming in. (How slack-jawed and unconscious these people had looked, they were like the people whose attention she had since—and earlier—tried to attract in bad dreams; the people who stayed outside urgency, blandly immune to her terror.) And then there he had been, their sensible child, standing directly across the street from the pavilion, his gaze fixed on the building's main doorway. They had run to him wildly—as if he were the parent and they were the children—and it had taken them a long time to get their fill of hugging and praising him.

But now Barbara's mind kept going round and round on the theme of the bush, and on Tim somewhere deep in it, every day in danger. It was such a misleading little phrase too, "the bush," it sounded so manageable and domestic, like "rosebush" or "here we go round the mulberry bush." Such a far cry from what it really was: hot and scratchy and dark, and spreading, for hundreds of miles, in some cases, all over the map. People thought of technology as producing monotony, but nature could produce monotony too, could be treacherously monotonous, like the treacherous monotonous bush. You could get lost in the bush and try to find your way back to some landmark: a bluff, a waterfall, a small lake with dead trees standing knee-deep in dead water. But then when you found it, it would only turn out to be a mirage, a new landmark. The bush was a mad maze made by God—there were a hundred thousand waterfalls, each one of them an exact replica of the one preceding it, and hundreds of thousand of little bluffs, and thousands upon thousands of small clearings with a few birches and poplars grouped in their middles, and then every ten minutes or so there would be another lake spiked with its small family of drowned trees.

The sound of the front door being slammed made Barbara wake up. Mitzi, it must be, back from Melanie's.

"Mit? Can you come up here for a minute?"

But when Mitzi stood in her doorway, she couldn't think of a thing to say to her.

"Were you asleep?"

"Yeah. I just thought I'd lie down for a minute or two and the next thing I knew I was dreaming." She sat up and reached for her blouse. She could see Mitzi trying not to stare at her breasts. She pulled the blouse on and self-consciously did up her buttons. She didn't want to do them up too fast, she didn't want Mit to think she was saying to her: Don't stare at them, for God's sake. And so she quickly said, "I had a weird dream."

"What happened in it?"

"I was looking for someone." (She'd been looking for Tim.) "It was a sort of pasture with a barbed-wire fence all around it. And far off in the distance I could see some trees that I thought were spruce trees but then someone was laughing and saying, 'No, no, those are called bruce trees.'"

"That's pretty weird."

"I guess I must have been thinking of your dad."

But Mit only said, "Barb?"

"Yuh?"

"You think I should try that thing that you tried when you were a kid?"

"You mean the breast thing?"

"Yeah."

Barbara hesitated.

"My dad says my mum's breasts were sort of average, maybe even a bit on the small side. . . ."

Barbara was ashamed of how glad it made her to hear this. She said, "Sure, Mit—why not? I was only hesitating for a minute because I was thinking you might get embarrassed if you forgot you weren't alone and did it over at Melanie's. Or at some other friend's place."

"But we've already talked about it. Mel wants to try it out too."

Down in the kitchen, the phone started to ring.

Mit clattered down to it in her little brown sandals, but by the time she'd grabbed it and cried hello into the receiver the caller had hung up.

Ring again, damn you, prayed Barbara, sliding her feet into her flip-flops, but the house only stayed filled with the swish and tick of a windy late afternoon in midsummer.

While they were washing the dishes after supper, Mitzi said, "Knock-knock," and Barbara said, "Who's there?"

"Barb."

"Barb who?"

"Barbed wire."

"Brilliant."

"And it can stand for Barb Dwyer too."

"Yes, I can see that. Double brilliant."

"I got the idea from your dream."

"From my dream?"

"You said there was a barbed-wire fence all around the bruce trees."

It was a maudlin thing to think, but sometimes Barbara wondered if Bruce, driving down the night highway toward home, ever felt a momentary terror that he would come back to find yet another wife dead. She didn't think it would be a thing she could ever ask him. And then she imagined the opposite: he was killed, killed on the highway, and someone was saying to someone, "Just imagine, she married a widower, and then in less than a year she was a widow herself."

She picked up the paper and tried to read it, but nothing stayed with her, her heart was too primed in an unpleasant way for the upheaval and deep tread of tire in gravel. Let everything be all right. But what if he was late because he was having an affair with someone? What if he'd already been back in the city for three hours and was over at this person's apartment right this minute? Who, though? Anyone. His secretary. Arlene, the nurse from the wedding. Malcolm. Old heart-stopping suspicions, left over from the Eduardo days. But then she reminded herself that even with luck it would have to be a long trip: the flight back to Temagami in the seaplane, then the drive down to North Bay. Which would be where he'd have to stop for his dinner. And then the much longer drive south.

A little after eleven she went upstairs to take a shower. She shampooed her hair in a hurry because she kept hearing what sounded like the ringing of the phone beneath the ringing of the water, but when she turned off the taps the house was still silent.

She stepped out of the shower stall, dripping and listening.

More nothing.

The short nightgown she pulled on over her wet hair made her think of a nightgown she'd had when Tim was a baby—its band of pink and grey smocking—the way pablum used to get hardened in some of the smocked parts.

But as she was coming down the dark stairs again, she heard a car door being slammed shut. She ran quickly down to the hallway in her bare feet, in too much of a hurry to bother to take the precaution of peering out through the side window and turning on the porch light.

When she drew open the door, a dark hulk stood on the doorstep, a great black-bearded bear, his unzipped windbreaker looking as splayed and shrunken as a cockeyed white nylon bolero. "Feed me something," he said.

They went down to the dark kitchen together.

"Was everything all right?"

"It was fine. He knew lots of people there."

"Did he? That's wonderful." She turned brightly toward him in the dark. "How many?"

He flicked on the light. "I exaggerated just a bit. He knew two other kids."

"Two's enough," she told him. She lifted the cast-iron pan down from its hook. If he likes them, she thought. "How many kids in his cabin?"

"Six. And their counsellor seems to be quite a decent young person too. Plays the flute and has acne. And you should have seen Tim when we were flying in on the plane—he was just so elated."

Barbara felt a power surge in her heart at the thought of Tim in the plane. "So thank you for making me let him go then."

"Don't mention it," he said and he came up behind her and with his left hand lifted her short nightie so that his free hand could slide down the back of her underpants. She leaned back against him, the pressure of his spread fingers a sweet consolation to her while he was kissing her lightly on the back of her neck, like a husband. And then while she was scrambling eggs with green onions, breathing in the vapour from their fine oniony sizzle, she told him the story about Mitzi and her breasts. When she'd finished it she said, "But now I feel as if I've been disloyal to her. Swear you won't let on you know anything."

"Sure I swear. What kind of an idiot blabbermouth do you take me for anyway?"

After Bruce had fallen asleep, Barbara stayed awake, listening to the still night. She was sleeping (or trying to sleep) while sharing a house with two people she didn't even know one year ago. If she had passed them in the street last September she would have thought: father, daughter, but she wondered if she would even have noticed them all that terribly much. She tried to imagine what sort of person she would have become if she had never married Eduardo, never given birth to Tim, never left (or been left by) Eduardo, never met Bruce. A woman alone with no dependents. No one to pray for. She was convinced that she would have been hard-hearted, secretly unsympathetic, without the simple (or complicated) decency to imagine other people's pain. Of course some people never even needed to marry, have children: they already had hearts and souls, you could see it in their eyes. Knowing that life was a tragedy, they were prepared to be kind. And so it did seem to her that it was possible that people in general (and married people in particular) had got it all wrong—and that marrying, or marrying again, was not after all a mark of fine emotional health, but only a kind of metaphor for entering life again and again because you continued to be in need of karmic correction. During the period between husbands, people who were married did seem to be a bit smug. Did seem to be saying: "I chose! I was chosen!" But if you were married and smug (or perhaps even if you were married and weren't smug), too much could be taken from you. Everything you loved. She pictured Tim at camp, brushing his teeth at the kind of pump they would have at a boys' camp in the wilderness, rinsing out his mouth with a few ounces of well water that he'd pumped into a battered tin cup. She could see him so clearly, her shyly dignified child. He was a small dot on a map—on a clearing the sunlit green mapmakers used when they wanted to indicate clearings. She felt it would take all of her breath and the pure will of her heart to keep him safely there, on the sunny side of the map. But at the same time she couldn't help wondering if it had occurred to Bruce, flying into the bush, to feel what she also felt: that from the point of view of their being kept under surveillance, the wrong child had been packed off to camp. Now they would have to snatch what love they could get the times Mit wasn't around to monitor them with the occasional ominous teenager look. It seemed to Barbara that this must be why she'd imagined a more romantic and in fact even a teenage-homecoming scene down in the kitchen—Bruce pushing her up against the wall and then the two of them kissing the way two adolescents might kiss: as if they'd just invented kissing. But at the same time as if they could guarantee, for both their children, safe passage through all of life.

TWO WOMEN: THE
INTERVIEWS

DRIVING DOWN THE HIGHWAY toward Hope Lonetree's painting
hut Delphine conjures it up: low little barn-red studio set down
in the same bluff and pasture country she's driving through right
now. And there's a dense fog this afternoon too, just as there was
on the first morning. She drives cautiously along in it, now and
then taking quick little squints to the right to try to catch a
glimpse of the Lonetree mailbox, and now at last here it is, and
just beyond it there's the sharp turn onto a ramp of tall weeds
and grasses, then the bumpy descent to the new studio with its
smell of raw paint in the mist.

Hopey, Hope's friends call her. Or so she says. But would she
even have any friends? She surely only has admirers, detractors,
minions, false friends—at least this is what Delphine thinks as she
parks the car to the right of the barn and its stand of sunflower

stalks, their heavy heads bowed in the damp afternoon. A deranged barking comes next, followed by Hope's hyperactive black dog, then by Hope herself, making her frowning way out into the day and looking even younger, if possible, than she looked before. How old would she be? She could be sixty-eight, sixty-nine, or she could be close to eighty. Here and there she has liver spots, in among all the freckles, and this afternoon she's wearing a black dashiki over a pair of burgundy slacks and her rusted black hair is still longish, girlishly curly. "So here you are then."

Delphine says she's sorry she's late, but she was afraid to drive too fast in the fog.

"You call this a fog? This is a mere mist, my darling."

Mist, pissed, thinks Delphine, following Hope up the three shallow steps into her studio. Because this is what irritated her most about the earlier interview with Hopey—her hungry need to have the last word.

They sit down at the long table, just as before—the studio kitchen, off to their left, smelling of the kind of raspberry jam Delphine remembers from summer camp, the kind with much too much pectin in it. This time she has her tape recorder with her and so she unbuckles it from its case, clicks it on while the second instalment of Hope Lonetree's story comes tumbling out: trip to Paris in '32 (which would make her a great deal older than sixty-nine), year at art school in London in '34, lover killed in Spain in '36, second lover shot down in the Battle of Britain, whole long string of lovers. And no husband, no children (no hostages to fate), but the good looks, the energy, the braying vitality that could all add up to a woman who might have lovers still.

Delphine only half takes it all in, she's so busy dashing off little notes in her notebook: B of B with a black cross under it for the shot-down lover, description of paintbrushes stuck into a green glass jug that Hope must have spatter-painted or left too near an easel, smell of turpentine along with the smells of paint and jam and Hope Lonetree's sweet lame old dog who seems to suffer from a kind of halitosis of the whole body as he sniffs at Delphine's right foot, then sniffs a bracelet of damp little nose kisses all around her right ankle. After this he trots down to the bathroom at the end of the studio to noisily lap water out of the toilet bowl and then on his way back makes a beeline for her foot once again, but changes his mind and proceeds to lick her left hand, leading her to make a mental note to herself to be sure to wash it before she eats the cookies that Hope will in all likelihood be serving with tea.

Fifteen minutes later, when Delphine can in fact hear Hope assembling the tea things out in the kitchen, the dog again comes over to her with his urgent mournfulness and sniffs at her notebook. "I'm writing about *you*, Doggo," she whispers down to him, and swinging the notebook well out of his reach she adds a quick postscript: "The whites of his eyes are red, but at the same time his eyes are bizarrely human-looking—he has a distrustful, human way of looking at you over his shoulder, which is very odd, for his personality"—he is pantingly trying to sniff at the notebook again—"is extremely gentle and friendly."

Over tea, Hope talks obsessively about her more recent sexual conquests, describing in detail a weekend she once spent with a Canadian poet in Mexico City (she calls it a "dirty weekend," an expression Delphine particularly dislikes, for some reason), then follows this story with a much more rambling recounting of two weeks spent in Dublin with a man who had "the filthiest mind in all of Ireland." Delphine sits spreading one slice of cornbread after another with salty country butter, and then drinks, like a woman dying of thirst, five cups of tea. The word "filthy" doesn't make her think of anything sexual; it makes her think of something filmy and nylon drying out in a little bathroom where the chrome fixtures keep giving off weak little flashes of themselves in a soap-scented, dim interior. And if anyone ever uses the word "unsavoury" in a sexual sense it only makes her think of glum men in long aprons, frying lamb chops and onions in spices and rancid oil.

The dog comes over to her again, pushes his nose between her legs with great friendly firmness and then simply parks it there, as if this is the only place in the world in which he can think his deep thoughts. His calmly resting nose makes Delphine feel oversexed, but possibly she's really only feeling this way because of all of Hopey's talk about men. Or because of the full-ness of the moon somewhere up there in the sky behind all the fog. Or maybe she's starting to get her period. (Maybe this is why Hope Lonetree's dog is finding her so appealing.) She pours herself another cup of tea and looks around at the paintings, stacked like cards against walls and easels, and begins to feel she admires them less than she did on her earlier visit, even though, objectively speaking, they can't have changed. But then she's all at once afraid that Hope will be able to read her mind, and so she says, "I've been meaning to ask you . . . about the name Lonetree. Is it an aboriginal name? I was wondering if it might be Micmac perhaps, or Iroquois. . . ."

But Hope says that her family is Irish. "From way back. Along with the statutory bits of bastard English and Welsh." And then she says that she's just going to nip upstairs for a minute to fetch herself a jacket.

Delphine is feeling a bit chilled herself, in her India print skirt and a gauzy white midriff blouse made out of a frail embroidered cotton, and so while Hope is upstairs she pulls on her own jacket—black leather windbreaker, last nod to youth—and walks around the studio to visit her favourite pictures once again: the one of the supermarket cart parked on the lawn of a cathedral— a pale-green snake of garden hose coiled up inside the cart, its nozzle aimed at a bed of tall cardinal-red tulips; a prairie landscape of a half-platter of pale grass in a reddish field; wide bands of yellow mustard flowers making miles of wet green fields look flooded with sunlight even though the leaden skies show the day as overcast and maybe even lightly raining. The dog follows her from picture to picture, but now he's poking and nuzzling at her from behind. "Hey," she says in a low lover's voice, turning to place a hand on his forehead and then holding it firmly there as if testing his brow for a fever. Then she starts to stroke back the pure perfect silk of his fur. "Why, sweetheart," she says. And means it. It's been a while since her body has been honoured with this much attention. Lately, in fact, her life has been one loss after another—Doug and Emma taking off for university three weeks ago (Doug as a freshman, Emma as a sophomore) and then the following weekend her best friends Becky and Steve moving to the other end of the country. It occurs to her that this is why she applied for the Arts Page job at her local paper—she wanted to extend (however briefly) her circle of acquaintances, wanted to crouch with her little notebook on the corner of one life, another life.

But what kind of education out in the world can Hope Lonetree have found, growing up when she did? There must only have been hints, innuendo. Even as late as the early sixties, there was nothing. At least there was nothing if you were naive, as Delphine believes she herself was, and didn't know where to look. No, there was nothing, and worse than nothing: bracing articles in the women's magazines designed to make young wives feel ashamed and abnormal if they didn't have an orgasm at the exact same instant as their husbands. The Big O: Delphine recalls reading a whole book about it once, about passion synchronized, about how vital it was for husbands and wives to achieve it. She remembers being three days away from her twenty-first birthday and anxiously skipping her way through this intimidating book at the public library while at the same time trying not to think of other married couples she knew. Or knew to see—the ones who would sit in glamorous silence while they listened to other young husbands and wives foolishly reveal their innocence in too much drunken babble and talk. How anxiously envious these reserved and condescending husbands and wives used to make her feel! They were always the ones who seemed to be wiser, more whole, more sexually deft, older. She felt she was thinking of it (and them) all the time, finally, that magic moment, but even so, she never once spoke of it to Jackson and he never once spoke of it to her.

And then one night when they were both too tired to care if it happened or not, instead of Jackson coming first and Delphine hurrying like a flustered servant to catch up, the magic synchronization occurred, and after that it was just so embarrassingly easy—as embarrassingly easy as all newly mastered enterprises come to be. And now there are even thousands of books and articles on this and other sexual subjects—books of questionnaires that women have filled out, and she does sometimes read them. For revelations, not boasting. But why? Because it's becoming more and more important for her to know something—not that the world is a benevolent place, exactly, that's asking too much, but that there really are people out there who are willing to let you know what they know. Sexual uneasiness, sexual happiness. The ones she wants to steer clear of are the ones who can't seem to stop letting their little flashes of triumph show, the numbers ladies, the ones who can't stop rattling their sexual credentials, the Hope Lonetrees of Now.

Delphine's mother analysed Jackson's handwriting before Delphine and Jackson got married. "He'll keep a tight grip on the purse strings but he'll always be faithful to you." But this had turned out to be not true, or at least half not true: he did keep a tight grip on the purse strings and he was spectacularly unfaithful to her. He couldn't help it, he said, women threw themselves at him. And it was clear to Delphine that this was so. But he must also have given them signals—must have dropped little hints to let women know he was theirs for the taking. She suspected that he complained about her too—that with other women he became a more dashing version of his everyday self: enigmatically moody, hard done by. Helpless, enlarged by their adoration, he must have brought out what was corrupt and strategically maternal in them. One of them, Josie (who for a time had pretended to be Delphine's best friend) had even stalked him, driving around in her dying Peugeot and waiting for him to walk out through the main gates of the university where he taught undergraduate history on Tuesdays and Thursdays. Weak-eyed, deeply tanned, she had squinted against the evening sun while she'd driven her dusty little car barefoot (this was according to Jackson, when he confessed it all to Delphine several weeks later), and then she'd chauffeured him around the city looking for places where they could sit and talk. But Delphine had (in anguish) imagined these parts of the city as the more pastoral parts, green urban bowers where they would whisper and kiss.

But even before the appearance (and subsequent disappearance) of Josie, Delphine used to brood over the fact that she and Jackson hardly made love at all any more. It was after they were perfectly synchronized that this began to happen, not long after the Big O. It was as if they couldn't bear to live under the sun of so much sexual happiness. It got to be so that it was only six times a month, some months only four or five. Finally Delphine began to record the nights on the kitchen calendar. At first she decided her code word would be "salt," but how would she ever explain to Jackson why she was needing to buy salt five times a month? And so in the end she'd used milk, and then added (like ingredients) whatever other words happened to be necessary at the time: light bulbs, Kleenex, six nectarines.

Before Delphine leaves, Hope Lonetree takes her on a tour of her vegetable garden. They walk up and down the verdant damp spill of it, checking on the progress of snow peas and green beans while garden saliva (sometimes with a sting in it) attaches itself to Delphine's bare ankles.

Hope bends to pull out a few misty weeds, then startles Delphine by linking arms with her to say, "You're so mild! Don't you ever get angry?"

Delphine can feel herself blush. And she can feel anger too, leaping inside her, a fish to the light. She gathers, as she's sure almost anyone would gather, that "mild" is Hope Lonetree's euphemism for "sexless." She says, "Oh, I can be vicious." She is thinking of the way she printed c + c (for "cold and conceited") under the B of B for Battle of Britain. She's also deciding that Hope is actually not a sexual person at all—she's only able to fool people into thinking she's sexy because she's just so obnoxiously vital.

But by now the obnoxiously vital Hope's thoughts have already jumped on to something else. "Come see my pretty little henhouse and we'll find you some eggs."

Before their children were born, Jackson and Delphine lived in a high-rise in a little park not far from a bandstand that looked out over the river. Their apartment was high up, or at least high up for their little town, up on the ninth floor, up above even the tallest of the trees in front of their building, but in winter the shadows of the tree branches would be magnified by the streetlights and thrown onto the hills of frost-fog that would form in the lower halves of the windows. One night while Jackson was working late at the office, Delphine sat in the darkened living room and watched what looked like the antler-shadows of a rocking-horse reindeer rocking back and forth in one of the cold steam-hills on the freezing glass. Antlers that were in reality tree branches, knobbed by ice and rocked back and forth in the cold wind below. Delphine was rocking too, thinking about Jackson while rocking in the rocking chair and feeling mesmerized by distrust. It was after midnight and he still wasn't back yet. She got up and went to their bedroom window to look out at the clear night. The black highway winding among hills of snow made her think of a picture in a songbook from childhood—the song the picture went with was "O Little Town of Bethlehem" and the illustration had shown a city in moonlight, a city of mosques that her child's unsophisticated eye had seen as a city of igloos. But then the line "How still we see thee lie" came to her and with macabre precision attached itself to an image of Jackson lying dead on the highway. She should fear for his safety instead of always suspecting him! Or so she told herself as she opened the window and breathed in the clear air of the perfect moonlit night. But then her

heart skipped a beat because she could hear the rustling of rain.
Rain in the leaves. But there were no leaves. And there was a
moon. So it was only the wind then—the wind moving among
the ice-encased tree branches and making them rustle like rain.

She was pretending to read when she heard Jackson come in.
She looked at her watch: five to one, then heard him run a glass of
water out in the kitchen and was ashamed that she felt only a
pathetic relief. He at the very least could have phoned to tell her
he'd be late. She heard him come down the hall. Often, when he
was very late, she would call humbly out, "Was the driving terribly
awful?" but this time she decided not to help him, let him be the
one to speak first. Besides, what would be the point of calling out
such a question on such a clear winter night? She turned the page
of her book primly, seeing nothing. But he didn't speak, and when
she turned around to say hello she found herself face to face with a
man with a black hood pulled all the way down over his head. She
made a terrified gasp-whimper, heard a voice say, "The hangman
cometh." And then Jackson pulled off the hood, a smile ready and
waiting as the hood exposed it. And it wasn't a hood at all, as it
turned out, it was only the long black stocking cap he wore the
nights he went skiing. But in the moment before she had known
that the man under the hood was Jackson, all the major arteries
leading to her heart had felt destroyed by terror. And so it was also
at this moment that she'd discovered the fierce unforgivingness of
the word "ever." As in (while pounding her fists all over Jackson's
chest): "Don't you ever ever ever ever *ever* do anything like that to
me again! You *hear* me? Not *ever!*"

By the time the foggy afternoon has turned itself into early
evening Delphine is on her way home from Hope's studio and

decides to stop in at a highway café for a quick bite to eat. From a tired young waitress who has a kind, almost middle-aged face, she orders a slice of pumpkin pie. This girl's eyes remind her of Emma's eyes, they seem to carry so much intelligent tenderness for the world. In spite of everything. Delphine eats her pie slowly, half-reading a newspaper, but all the time she's reading or pretending to read she's really thinking of one of the answers in a book of sex questionnaires that she keeps beside her bed like a Bible: a woman talking about how she loves to be shoved up against a wall by her lover, with clothes on, and then to feel his whole hand against her.

Hope Lonetree is only the fifth person she's interviewed so far. The first person she interviewed was a local novelist who kept telling her he was a loner, a private person, that he loathed giving interviews, and yet there he was, in two of the magazines and three of the newspapers she happened to pick up during the course of the following two weeks, smiling shyly and saying the most magnificently humble things to his interviewers. She wishes she could interview him again, then she could call her piece THE UBIQUITOUS RECLUSE.

She's a secret writer herself, which is why she in particular studies the writers as she sits perched with her notebook and watches them as they listen to their own voices talk. Watches them do little checks on their modesty thermostats. She takes invisible notes at the same time that she's making the official notes on the page.

After Delphine and Jackson went through a bad period following one of his affairs, Delphine started to keep tabs on him. So that on the nights he told her he had to go finish up a few things at the office she'd sometimes get so tense about the possibility of his not having gone there after all that she'd give in to the temptation to phone him with a list of things for him to pick up on his way home. The sick relief she would feel when he would pick up the phone was something she taught her voice to conceal. She'd say, "We're out of cream and could you pick up some garlic butter too? Just one of those little bricks of it, in the green foil—" And she would be so grateful that he was there and taking down the list that after they'd said goodbye she'd sit on the bench by the phone with her knees hiked up, and bite one knee, then the other knee. They'd also taken in two boarders that year, a courtly history student from Nairobi whose name was Wamae, and a studious goddess from Stockholm whose name was Bibi, and not long after Wamae's and Bibi's departures they'd been visited, in succession, by the two mothers—or, as they preferred to call them when they were describing the two visits to their friends—the two mothers-in-law: Delphine's mother-in-law first, Jackson's mother-in-law second. So that the night they'd taken Jackson's mother-in-law to her plane (Final Mother Night), they were filled with such euphoric gratitude that they drove fast back from Uplands airport, rushed Dougie and Emma through their baths and bedtime story, then wolfed down hunks of cheese and quick mugs of wine. The bed they had ended up on was not their own bed, but Wamae's. (And, after Wamae's departure, the bed of first one mother, then the other mother.) It was the most amazing time they ever had together, sexually—depraved, tolerant. It had taken years and years after that night for them to get a divorce.

Now Delphine is back in the car again and the green Exit signs are coming at her as fast as flash cards, waking her up, and behind the Exit signs stand the upright dark trees of the forest, and on a far windy dark hill a radio tower, a red eye languorously winking shut, winking open. But after a short time there's open country again, then the low glow of the city, seen across the flat land. She pretends she's driving out of prehistory toward it, and as she comes into the stale sprawl of its outskirts she pictures herself continuing on in her new job, interviewing people. But she can never imagine it for long without also picturing herself as the one being interviewed. Something about sex. She sees herself sitting at a table in a sunlit café, her eyes wisely alive with a smiling easy calm. "After all," she is saying, "Someone needs to speak for the sexually shy, and I feel eminently qualified to be the one to do it."

FREAKISH VINE
THAT I AM

IN THE BLURRED MORNING the doorbell, then Bruno in his big
boots thundering down the stairs to the street door to let
Norman in.

Breathlessly furious with myself for having overslept, I poked
my nightgown into my trousers, then hurried down the hallway,
breathing in the smell of fog and fried ham. And then as I was
ducking into the kitchen to pack Bruno his lunch I ran into Bruno.

Norman came up the stairs then too, his overcoat exhaling a
great misty breath of cold air. He stationed himself in the kitchen
doorway and smiled down at me as he watched me slice tomatoes and Havarti cheese. I wanted to say to him: The more you
smile, damn you, the more I feel cross.

But he had something to tell me: "You seem to have a sock
protruding from one of your trouser legs."

I craned around to squint down at the backs of my slippers and saw a tongue of black legging drooping behind me. "Oh Lord. Part of my tights."

"Sorry, by the way, that I woke you up."

I said in a cool voice, "I was getting up anyway."

"I was just thinking of the family that was."

I pretended not to hear. Things couldn't be going all that well for him and Dorie if he was getting all nostalgic about the old days. But then Dorie was constantly sick, according to Bruno. And according to Tom she was an elaborate cook. Lethally elaborate: sugar and salt and white pastry flour.

Bruno came back into the kitchen, his backpack hugged high to his chest. He was dressed more conservatively than usual to go off for the day with his father: jeans and the shiny black jacket of a second-hand tux. No more black derby, either, since Norman could not abide any sort of hat on the head of a male descendant. "Food," said Bruno, in a gloomily gleeful cartoon monster voice. "Is it ready?"

Norman smiled at Bruno's shaved head with nervous affection. Or was it nervous condescension? He bowed to Bruno, half-mocking. "My son the convict."

"Yes, Father, I am a maniac."

I wrapped Bruno's sandwiches in slick butcher-shop paper and when I handed him the packet he buckled it into his backpack. And then because I was still feeling a bit chilled I went down the hall to my bedroom to tie on my robe.

I could hear Norman's footsteps coming right behind me. I hoped he was only going into the bathroom. But then in a dull panic I thought of the way I'd snowed talcum powder all over the ugly mulberry fur of the bath mat. And worse: the daily debris that Bruno and I lived with—jumble of toothpaste and shampoo tubes and old Kleenexes and earrings and Band-aids and waterlogged magazines and the toilet bowl needing a good thorough scour with Toilet Duck.

But I could hear that he was trailing me all the way down to my room.

And then he stood watching from the threshold as I drew on my old slinky black rayon robe, relic of our married days. I tied it on fiercely, not wanting to be looked at. I felt harsh. Go *away*, I wanted to say to him. This is my *bed*room.

But he continued to just stand there, taking note of the scatter of sandals and file folders and teacups and the soft hill of flowered panties down on the floor. He seemed to be feeling a kind of awed greed to take it all in.

Had your fill? I wanted to say to him.

"Look, Kris, I'm sorry to bother you with this, but would you mind if I used your phone for just a minute?"

I would have to allow him to come in then, to reach the phone, perched up on top of a tall stack of books. Irritably, I cleared a space for it down on my desk, set it down fiercely. It made a pinged bong. Probably it's not an important call *at all*, I thought. All he's really after is an excuse to snoop around in my life.

It was a call to his office.

I eavesdropped on it while I was brushing and then tightly pinning back my hair. And as I was watching him talk and listen, I could see his gaze moving over the quotes I'd tacked to the corkboard on the wall above my desk. I saw that his attention was being caught by the two quotes that, as it so happened, I least wanted him (or anyone) to see.

I kept trying not to watch him. I kept trying not to remember that the first one was about love being a shadow—a shadow with hooves that had run off like a horse. And the second one was:

> Freakish vine that I am,
> I prefer to reach for the light alone

I felt ashamed, watching his gaze rest on the first quote, on the second. How childish I must seem, I thought, tacking up adored quotes like a schoolgirl. And what if he thought that I was pining for *him*? What if he thought that the love that had run off like a horse referred to his former love for *me*? That would be a laugh. Of course if he decided it referred to some other man's love, he would feel contempt for me too. But wasn't I free to judge him as well? If I felt like it? His apparently unsuccessful marriage, his apparent loneliness, his apparently being at perpetual loose ends? His being perpetually hungry for company and hungry for love? But the fact of the matter is, the one whose possessions are being inspected is always the one who ends up feeling judged.

He set down the phone, still clearly trying to decode the story of my happiness or unhappiness from the writing up on the wall. Then he asked me what I was planning to do when Bruno left home.

"Find another place."

"Now that you're thinking of giving up your job at the paper, will you be able to afford another place?" He was staring again at the horse quote.

I said with a jaunty coldness (to cover my fear), "More easily than I can afford *this* place."

He went over to my window to look out at the trees and the fog. "Something I've never understood—why you'd live all these years just a short walk from the university and then never even bother to take even one single course there."

"What should I have taken a course in?"

"You could have done a B.A. in English, then an M.A., you could have done your doctorate, you could have taught English, you could have been a professor by now, had tenure. . . ."

"I have better things to do with my life than become a professor."

He asked me what. But at this merciful point he remembered to look at his watch and so I was left to follow him as he followed Bruno down the stairs to the street.

Down by the front door, I hugged Bruno goodbye. "Drive safely," I said.

The morning paper, rolled up and with an elastic band wound around it, was lying on the wet doorstep. Norman bent down to retrieve it. Then he handed it to me with one of his uncertain small bows. "I don't know if you heard me back up there in the kitchen. I was just saying that I was thinking of the family that once was."

Again I didn't respond.

"Time goes on," he said, stepping with an awful solemnity out into the cool foggy morning while Bruno, already on his way across the lawn to the car, glanced quickly back at him, not approving.

"Safe trip!" I called out after them, forgetting that I had already said it.

Bruno threw back at me over a shoulder, "Have no fear, Mother dear, we'll drive like the senile and truly deranged people we are." But he was looking happy enough, a young man taking pleasure in change, a new landscape, the potential it would give him (when he looked back on it later) for sardonic remarks.

Norman did not wave. He was looking as if he had briefly considered it but then had sensibly decided against it. His grey overcoat looked expensive, a kind of grey suede. It had sloping shoulders and a womanly yoke at the back and it fell in such graceful folds that it made me think of a suede nightgown. He's lost his judgement, I thought.

After the car had turned the corner at the top of the street, I went up the stairs to make myself tea. The bouquet of wild mauve asters down on the low black table was done for. I emptied the foul water out of the jug and wrapped the slimy stems in a page of newspaper displaying a long row of pale women in delicate slips. A chore particularly suited to the fogged-in chill of the morning. I felt how absolutely empty and still the apartment was, how much it smelled of dead dishcloth.

Then I sat and sipped at my tea. And after a time I remembered my tights, the droopy black tongue of them, ludicrously dragging behind my left foot. I thought of Norman's being so nostalgic about our past, and again wondered if it could mean trouble at home. I did not want to be responsible, ever again, for his happiness. Or for his unhappiness either. And then I began to pull, with a certain comic peevishness, at the toe of the tights. The act provided the stilled aftermath of the car's departure with its moment of event—I pulled and pulled until I'd yanked all of the left stocking-leg out of the left leg of my trousers. It came out like a black cotton tapeworm, like a black ligament, made me feel like a conjuror doing a flawed demonstration of a slow-motion trick.

Saturday shopping: but it had to be done. I walked out to the market, pushed my shopping cart up and down crowded aisles.

There were three people in line ahead of me at the check-out depot, and while I was waiting my turn I flipped through pages of starlets with enlarged smiling faces and abnormally short legs, the consequence of their having been photographed from stairwells and balconies. A surprising number of these women were wearing red crêpe dresses that appeared to have had their padded red crêpe shoulders sprinkled with red sugar. But now the line was starting to move forward and so I loaded my Feta cheese and marmalade and rice onto the conveyor belt behind the towers of beer cans being assembled by the person preceding me. I waited, dreaming; looked out the window. The fog had lifted, now there was sun on the leaves of the spindly trees in front of the market and I could almost feel a man's hand stroking back my hair so that he could look into my eyes and then I was thinking of how when Bruno left home and the child support payments stopped I'd have only the pathetic income from my job on the paper and so I'd have to go to night school and learn how to teach English to immigrants or maybe even travel to Japan to teach English to Japanese businessmen and live in polluted Tokyo in a tiny apartment with rice-paper walls, alone and truly lonely in another country, which made me recall that when Tom and Bruno were babies, Norman and I had lived a surprisingly Japanese life, having developed a passion for Japanese rice-paper lamps and Japanese movies. Even our dining-room table was a lacquered square of black wood that we'd had to kneel at to eat. And the food that we ate at it must often have been Japanese too, because when Norman's mother came to visit and had to kneel to eat with us—she was at that time a tall and fair Polish woman in brown tartan slacks kneeling at the low table and simmering, although we didn't yet know it, at least not until the final night of her visit when she threw her fork down on the floor and cried out, "Why can we never have potatoes in this house? Why does it always have to be *rice, rice, rice?*" In the Japanese movie we'd taken her to after dessert—a last-minute (and possibly totally inappropriate) treat to make amends for the rice-diet—a young woman was running bare-breasted through a field of moonlit blades of tall grasses photographed to look like a harvest of wind-blown knives—running toward a lover and away from some terror—and the soundtrack was filled with the bumpy and gasping sound of desperate running along with the metallic and also frightening sound of the disturbed grasses, a harsh, feudal whoosh—but now the cashier's voice was calling out to me with the total, and when I looked up I saw that the girl was mocking me—was rolling her eyes while waiting and smirking and in the process also giving my face and hair and old sweater and lipstick-less lips a condescending once-over. The moment I understood it was real mockery, I felt a surge of nausea in my heart and could not even think. I could only fumble the money out of my waist-pouch and try to look courtly and neutral. But the girl seemed to want to be sure her message had been received and so continued to hold the same insolent foot-tapping smile in her eyes, a smile that said, You're no one, you're a loser, you're so much of a loser that even I, a lowly cashier, am not afraid to let you know you're a loser, and as she handed me my change I glanced up to read the incised name on her green plastic name card and when I saw what it was I knew it had to be one of God's or the devil's little jokes because the name on the card was Charity.

But how was it that even idiots knew how to wound? Knew (as if born to it) the whole choreography of malice? So I happened to be looking a bit scruffy and vague on this particular morning, but wasn't I only minding my own business? And at this I recalled the times that Bruno and Tom had been hurt by louder and more sadistic children and I remembered how I had longed to viciously slap the gleeful visitor children, longed to scream at them to go home and never dare to come back to play at our house again. And not only because the children who had been hurt were my own children, but because they too had only been minding their own business (the business of childhood) and so had been innocently singing or whisperingly playing with their precarious cities of blocks. It was on behalf of my children as children that I wished I'd had the presence of mind to say some terrible thing to the spiteful little cashier with the vulgar eye make-up and the dusty overpermed hair even though she had barely been beyond childhood herself. If I could have just stood there and calmly watched her die! And yet I knew that within a few hours the heartbroken venom that was making me feel gnawed at and ashamed would become diluted, would leave me, and besides, I didn't want her to die, I wanted her to live and even to live long. Live long and suffer. Learn what it was to be jeered at, downfallen.

But then another surprise: a block before the turn-off to my street a young man who came walking toward me smiled at me with a quick male sweetness that seemed to see with a true sexual tenderness straight into my heart. "Hi ya," he said, as if he knew me, and even knew me well. "How ya doing?" And although I said hi to him too, what I really wanted to call out after him was "Thank you!"

Low male voices down in the dark lane, sound of a car door slamming shut. Which made me picture Norman slumped at the wheel, tired at the end of his journey in his nightgowny coat.

Then another sweet sound: his car taking off.

I turned up the heat under the stew I'd put on one of the back burners for Bruno, dealt out the straw mats. I was glad it was too late for him to go off to be with his friends, I so much hated lying awake till all hours to make sure he got safely back before dawn. I called out, "So how was it?"

"The campus at Concordia is just nothing! It doesn't even exist!"

I ladled his stew into one of the cereal bowls.

He came into the kitchen and sat down at his place. "The university is just a bunch of office buildings in the middle of downtown." He blew on his stew, then turned his spoon sideways to break open one of the chunks of cooked beef. "The city is beautiful though. It's got topography."

"Unlike Toronto?"

Toronto! *God,* he'd never want to go to school in Toronto. "But the funny thing about Montreal is that even though the food is supposed to be so superb there, it really wasn't all that great. We ate at this trendy goulash place, and the potatoes tasted like they'd steamed them in mothballs or something."

Soon he will leave home, I thought, and what will the robin do then, poor thing. I said, "What in the name of God was Dad going on about this morning?" And I mimicked Norman's voice saying "I was just thinking of the family that *was.*"

He'd noticed it too.

"I felt as if he was trying to court me or something."

He looked up at me, startled. I was certain it filled him with an old childhood terror (or both wish and terror)—the possibility that his parents might feel drawn to each other once again. But what surprised me most was that in spite of everything, I did at least for a moment feel bizarrely wounded by what I was sure he was going to say next. And then he said it: "Oh, I didn't think *that,*" he said.

THROUGH THE FIELDS
OF TALL GRASSES

FROM THE TIME OF THEIR EARLIER and more innocent experiments: how they'd played a game called Husband and Wife which had involved sending their little sister Rebecca—sometimes she was their cook, sometimes she was their child—off on imaginary shopping trips. How when they'd heard her panting—her panting almost matching their panting—as she'd started to joyfully make her return climb up the stairs, they'd called out a new (and much longer and more gleefully random) list of things for her to trot back to the imaginary store for. How the more they had tried to trick and detain her, the more her distant stair-climbing panting had seemed to signal euphoria and goodwill and even a belief that they must be trying to improve the game for her by inventing even more imaginary foods for her to hunt down with her imaginary basket. "Buttons!" they had yelled down to her. "Balloons! Blue ones! A red bathing cap! Marmalade! Bananas!" And they'd been joined in cruel sibling glee by the sound of Becca's joyful panting breaths as she had once more changed direction and started to happily stamp away from them again, back down the stairs. It was almost comical to think of it—how the two of them had managed, out of desire and cunning, to keep all three of them happy. It was only the later memories that Caitlin found really disturbing, memories from when they were twelve and thirteen and no longer had Becca to distract them from their knowledge that what they were doing was in itself thrilling, a far cry from the pleasure they'd got out of playing tricks on a little sister. It was the real thing then, something they'd both wanted for its own sake. But there had been, in spite of all the really intense excitement, something shame-faced about it, as if they had been anointed by weirdness.

And they didn't even go all the way, they only rubbed so hard against each other that they forgot the world and wanted to forget it again and again. They didn't even think about their being brother and sister. If what they were doing was wrong, it was only wrong because it was sex, thought Caitlin, not because they were brother and sister. She was sure, in fact, that her mother, if she had known about it, would have preferred them to keep it in the family, to not do it with strangers. One night when two of their friends from the next farm were visiting and they were all necking down in the den (Caitlin with Harold and Kev with Colleen), their mother, walking by, had noticed that all the lights were turned out in that part of the house and so had also turned off the hall light and soundlessly eased open the den door and hidden herself behind the curtains and then jumped out at them—terrifyingly, out of the total darkness—yelling that they were bad children and that Harold and Colleen were to go home at once.

DULUDE

But Dr. Dulude surprises her—she is by this time in her thirties and married but childless—by not taking her confession about what happened between her and Kevin all that seriously. He shrugs one of his Gallic shrugs and lifts his palms, waiting for rain. "Fun and games, lots of children play them, no harm done. Naturally you and your brother would have been abnormally close since you were both partly raised by other families. What happened to you while you were living with the doctor and his family is perhaps significant though. All those enemas and nose-drops. *That* must have felt very invasive to a small child living far from home. . . ."

"Not really," she is tempted to answer, even though ordinar-ily she finds it next to impossible to resist even a minor oppor-tunity to wallow in self-pity. What she chiefly recalls about the nosedrops is squirming away, then being captured and held down on the big bed while the cold medicinal plop of the drops being dropped down her nostrils made the back of her brain and the arch of her throat sting. As for the enema, it may have been given to her only once—this would explain why she has such a vivid memory of it: her cold little bum poked into the air while she was kneeling on the warm white tiles of the bathroom floor, the cold trickle of water running like liquid ice down inside her as if it wouldn't stop till it came out of her mouth. But she also has memories of being given a winged pinafore to wear over a blue taffeta dress and calling the doctor and his wife Daddy Kingsley and Mummie Faith and every Saturday night being washed in the tub by Gloria, the doctor's daughter—Gloria's braids hanging down in the steam while she ticklingly creamed her fat little arms and legs with a fat cake of soap. Then Gloria would lift her out, wrap her in a big warm towel and run with her into Faith and Kingsley's bedroom to dump her onto their bed where they would play a game called Fisherman which would involve Gloria using two of Faith's hairnets to capture Caitlin's wet feet with while Caitlin would shriek with the triumphantly insane joy of childhood. What with all the capture and excitement and attention and pretty dresses, she had felt her life to be much superior to Kevin's. He had only been farmed out to a farm family—people whose house Faith and Kingsley had driven her to visit one Sunday afternoon—a big square yellow house in a peony garden, cats all over the place. She had imagined Kev eating nothing but tapioca pudding there. But that was because of the family's name—Tapley or Tappett. They'd had a daughter named Ginger and some of the cats were ginger cats and Ginger had carried one of the cats around in her arms pretending it was her baby. Or her lover. Because although she'd rocked it in her arms and called it her baby, the way she said "Oh, baby" to it made her sound like a woman talking to a lover. Caitlin has a memory of being fussed over by a group of big girls of nine or ten and then being taken by the hand and led across a field to two trees that had a hammock like a giant red hairnet slung between them. She recalls staring, fascinated, as Ginger kept swinging back and forth in the hammock with the little ginger kitten half-hidden in her partly undone blouse while she tried to get it to suck on one of her nipples. For some reason Rebecca was there too, but Rebecca couldn't even have been born yet, that was why they'd been sent to live with other families in the first place, because their mother was pregnant with Rebecca and at the same time trying to help their father get his antique business off the ground.

Caitlin tells Dulude that she's certain Kevin feels guilt. "I know that now, even though we've never spoken of it, and do you know how I know it?"—she turns to him, fierce and imploring, her throat in pain from the humiliating wish to have him give her his total attention—"Because the whole time we were in high school he kept pushing me at other boys and then when they liked me"—but here she has to stop, force some calm into her voice before going on—"he couldn't stand it. He also used to make me feel so bad about the way I looked, and even though I know now it was out of guilt, I still—" But at this point she is obliged to abandon the sentence entirely. Instead she says in a much lower voice, "He'd run into me in the hallway outside the gym and say, 'I saw you sitting all by yourself in the cafeteria today at lunchtime again—Christ, you were all hunched up like an old woman. Try to cheer up and make some friends, okay?'"

To which Dulude replies, "Of course we do know from Freud that children who are sexually active during the latency period tend to experience difficulties later in life. . . ."

And to Caitlin's "Did he mean sexual difficulties?" his gloomy response is, "I believe he meant difficulties in every area."

HORSE

The summer Caitlin turned ten, there was a visitor to her parents' farm who played Horse with her. A flushed man in a navy blazer with a wiry gold crest on its breast pocket and a necktie that had a pattern of small silver crowns on it. He began by letting all the children have turns riding on his shoulders, but after a little while the others figured out that Caitlin was the only one who got taken for long runs and so they went off with their parents and this man's wife to go for a walk on the beach.

Horse and Caitlin were left to gallop through the fields of tall grasses that surrounded the house, snorting and prancing and shouting "Giddyap" to each other. Caitlin could feel the firm pressure of Horse's fingers on the fronts of her thighs, and on the insides of her thighs the funnier and even more exciting prickle of his neck-bristles. He pretended to dip her into a barrel of rain-water and she screamed. He let her use his divided necktie as reins and she started swatting him on the neck with one of the tie's floppy ends. He wheeled around then, in the field, and whinnied his way back to the house. At the door he jiggled her up and down for a bit and then pawed at the doorstep with his crêpe-soled loafers and produced two silly and fiercely magnificent snorts. The pulse Caitlin could feel inside herself, behind her panties, strengthened, tunnelled in. And at this point, Horse, as if he could read her mind, trotted into the house, looking, he told her, between snorts, for a pile of hay. He trotted over to the horsehair sofa. (Could this black itchy sofa be a pile of hay? If it could be, then it would all be all right. Anything could happen but it would still only be a game.)

Horse pawed the braided rug in front of the sofa. "Hay," he said. Or, possibly, "Hey." Then he revolved his neck in quick (but horse-like) half-circles in the dampening yoke of her panties; waited, it seemed, for some signal from her. Oh, do it. She swatted him smartly with one end of his tie, and at this he dumped her down on the sofa. He sat down then as well, beside the hip of her short skirt, and then he started to tickle her knees—the fingers of one hand did a soft-shoe shuffle on one of her knees, then danced off the curve of that knee, clicked heels midair to land dancing on the next knee. And all the time this was happening, all Horse's face revealed was what appeared to be an experimental lack of expression, as if his face had no knowledge of (or interest in) what his fingers were up to, down at her knees. And so she laughed and laughed. The face without life, the hay-itchy sofa, didn't they mean what was happening could keep going on? But then something clicked as the tickling fingers stopped dancing around her knees and a hard businesslike look mounted into the eyes and the fingers started to walk toward her panties. And as the fingers were walking—pretending to go slow but getting there—the whole face changed until it looked like a drowned-fish face, and at the sight of this drowned-fish face she jumped up off the sofa (for suddenly she could not bear one single thing about him, not his fishy eyes or his fishy breathing or the way he so fishily smelled of lemon tart and B.O.) and she fled from the house, her legs weakened by the sickened thrill of escape as she raced across three fields, up the long hill by the old barn, found Kevin.

They lay in the long grass up behind the old barn, up among the liver-spotted apples, the liver-spotted leaves, and she spilled out to Kev everything that had happened.

"Did he fuck you?"

"No," she whispered. "No, he didn't do that."

"Calm down, then."

They lay side by side in the long grasses, not speaking. When they heard their mother calling them for tea they didn't go. Kevin shimmied through the grass on his stomach till he reached a look-out point.

"Kevin! Caitlin!" they could hear their mother calling in the melodious voice she saved for the times company came.

But the next time something happened, Caitlin didn't have to run—she was sent off, banished. And the next time it happened, it happened with Kevin. Two weeks after her twelfth birthday, in the cedars, a good safe distance from the house. All summer long Kev had spent all his spare time out there, building a hut out of cedar logs. Caitlin had to walk through spruce and fir woods to get to the cedars; through forests that were tinderbox woodland cathedrals, fodder for forest fires, their slingshot twigs turned into dangerous kindling. And everything silent except for the sound of Kev's axe. When she got to where he was working she could see the shin-like look the cedar trees had when their bark was stripped down and could smell the sweet scent of torn tree skin. Kevin was gleaming and brown and also stripped down, at least to the waist. They were both too old for playing Husband and Wife, which didn't mean she didn't still want to. It even seemed to her that her heart was beating like a slow drum, in the wrong place, far too low for a heart to be.

She walked away from him, through a thicket of alders and shiny red bushes, trying to calm herself. She remembered how he had once said to her, "Calm yourself, then." But as she plunged through the bushes, their branches stroked her breasts and thighs, and then a crucial branch, like permission being given, nicked her. She turned and went back to him. She could tell by the way he was looking at her that he'd been expecting her to turn back. And she knew he was thinking what they'd both thought when they were children: nobody has to know. They wouldn't kiss or anything (that would be awful), it was just that they would both be able to take what they wanted, the way they used to when they were children, and so she walked over to him and he shoved her where she wanted to be shoved, against a tree, and they rubbed against each other violently. But she would have done anything with him—anything except kissing—and this anything feeling was also thrilling and made everything she'd ever wanted in her life (silver bike, silver oak-leaf bracelet with her name engraved on it) seem like nothing at all and was only spoiled by Kevin saying, "You go home now."

She started off, in shame and in sullen something or other. Gratitude? But if it was gratitude, it was a mean gratitude and made her feel a secret fury, as if she wanted to pay him back for something. And so although she started to go, she didn't get far. She loitered, inhaled the honeyed cedar fragrance of the languorous air, the high summer sense that anything goes. She came back to look at the hut he was building (she hadn't looked at it properly, before), stroked the creamy stripped wood, smooth as satin, admired his prowess with the axe.

"You only want more of *that*," he said to her. "That's why you're back here."

It was true. She wanted more of it.

"For Christ's sake, *go*," he said.

And so this time she went.

But very soon after this she also went downhill. Her golden nubility faded. She got religious, but not religious immediately enough to make a connection. Or not religious enough to deal with the guilt. Or too religious to deal with the guilt. Walking along the corridors at school she hid her breasts behind a bulky screen of books and notebooks.

"Hey, Lumpy!" the boys called out from their huddle near the lockers.

Not deceived.

SO RUDE AND SO WRONG

Caitlin is lying on the couch at Dulude's again. She is talking about incest and revelations of incest, they are everywhere now, has he noticed? "And I'm glad," she says in a vehemently grateful voice, "the more it all comes tumbling out, the better," but what it all makes her realize, she says, is how little she, personally, has suffered.

But Dulude doesn't like her to be noble, he thinks it's deceitful, and so he says in a voice that has a thousand irritated sighs tucked away in it, "But surely it's clear to you by now—we really have no interest, at least at this stage, in people who may have suffered more than you have. Let's just stick to the topic at hand here which is your own suffering."

Is this contempt? Contempt veiled by irony veiled by politeness? And what about the way he says "at this stage," as if she's at some primitive level of moral evolution and therefore a total egomania is not only tolerated but is also his actual prescription for her? She throws a swift deciphering glance back over her shoulder. But there is no eye-gloat, his face has the fallen look of a man who is only doing his job.

The fact of the matter is, she is always trying to figure out how to *be* with him. Either she whines more or less constantly or she doesn't whine enough. Sometimes she acts (or tries to act) as if she's much too normal to be here, everything in her childhood was fine, terrific, no problems, people were kind to her, they did their best. She thinks of someone saying (or writing? was it Thoreau?), "What demon possessed me, that I behaved so well?", and then, as if to spite herself, she actually says, "People were mainly awfully kind to me, they did their best. Even my mother, in her way, did what she imagined was best for her children—"

She twists around on the couch to peer back at him. His eyes are closed. Is he asleep? And isn't this exactly what she deserves, that he should be asleep? It would be a humiliation, but in a way she would be glad. For him not to have heard what she so unwisely just said. But she's afraid to whisper, "Are you asleep?" She's afraid he really is asleep, and that he won't answer. Or that he isn't asleep and will answer. And that when he answers he'll say—if he decides it's therapeutically useful to be cruel—"No, not asleep, only bored."

She toys with the idea of telling him that her husband finds the name Dulude absolutely hilarious for a man in Dulude's line of work. She feels an absolute longing to say to him, "My husband likes to say, 'Who—or should I say *whooom*—does he delude? *You*, I bet.'" Only the suspicion that some of his patients have already said the same thing to him, or possibly some even wittier version of the same thing, keeps her from it. And besides, Dulude (being Dulude) will not be amused and will be only too happy to prove it to her by bombarding her with testy little questions about the timing of such a comment—timing being invariably linked, in the mind of Dulude, to unacknowledged feelings of hostility on the part of the joke-teller—and so she instead says, "When I was nine or ten I was invited to spend a weekend at Faith and Kingsley's house in Saint John."

She does an anxious but also somewhat cynical squint, preparatory to turning to check up on him again. As she turns, he opens an eye and squints back. And so she feels it is probably safe to continue. The House of Enemas, he is probably thinking. Her father drove her to Saint John one hot Friday morning in early July, the ocean on their right, the ocean and the stomach-dropping smell of its brine and marshes all the way into the city. Already sick to her stomach from homesickness, she couldn't speak. And so her father did all the talking, trying to entertain her, but there were long periods of quiet too, when they both sat staring straight ahead, their eyes on the road.

Everything was too bright in Saint John, the grass on the lawn of Faith and Kingsley's house was too bright a green, and the flowers that smelled sweet or sour were too bright (orange and red), and Faith's smile was too brightly lipsticked in the painful bright city light. Caitlin's head hurt her and she was afraid she might need to throw up from all the brightness. Her father asked her if she wanted to go out and play in the garden while he had a quick cup of tea with Aunt Faith. This was what she was supposed to call her, now that she wasn't living with her any more.

And so she went out into the garden. But there, hitting her in the stomach, was the homesick-making smell of the ocean again, and all the clank and hiss of the city. I can't stay here, she thought, but she had no idea how she could ever say such a thing, it would be so rude and so wrong. She walked around and around the green garden. She walked up a little hump in the lawn and looked down at the lily pond and stared for a long time at the pads of lily leaves resting on much larger pads of green scum. The lily pond smelled stagnant, like the olives she remembered that Faith and Kingsley used to serve when she was small and they invited company to come over for drinks. She had taken a bite out of one of them once and had wanted to throw up. What if she had to eat them while she was here this time? Now that she was older, she might be expected to. The other bad food the pond smelled like was asparagus. Little limp logs of wet cooked asparagus rolled up in slices of white bread were also what Faith would serve to company sometimes for a treat. Faith's housekeeper made nice desserts, though—especially the one that looked like chunks of white foam and was flavoured with lemon. It was called Lemon Snow and you were supposed to pour custard over it out of a jug. Faith had to ring a little silver bell to signal to the housekeeper when it was time to bring

in the Lemon Snow. And although Caitlin liked the housekeeper, it always made her feel tense when she came bustling
into the dining room because while she was changing the plates
and pouring fresh ice water, no one would speak.

The person who made her really nervous, though, was
Kingsley. Once when she was still small, she got a big boil on
her bum, and her mother pulled down one side of her bloomers
to show the boil to Kingsley. Caitlin had twisted back to look
down at it too and had seen what looked like a very small breast
with a sore pink nipple on it. And in the middle of the sore nipple a blackhead. Kingsley had probed it with a finger and then
recommended an ointment that looked like green road tar. But
it had made her feel shy to have Kingsley looking at her boil—
she'd had to hug the bunched-up sides of her skirt tight up into
her armpits and then bashfully clench herself.

And then she had farted, even though she had tried with all
her might not to—a tiny fart like the peep of a chick. But her
mother had heard it and afterwards told her that she'd been
really ashamed of her. "Kingsley was embarrassed too," said her
mother. "But of course he was much too polite to give any indi-
cation of it. . . ." And then one morning a long time after her
mother had asked Kingsley to look at the boil, and even long
after Caitlin's parents had gone back to the country, Faith had
come up the stairs and said to Caitlin, "Guess who's downstairs?
And wants to see you?" And Faith had tied on her good shoes
for her and combed back her hair. When Caitlin had come
down to the living room, there were two very tall strangers who
reminded her of her father and mother. And then she saw that
they really were her father and mother, and so she ran to her
father's leg to hug it, but then decided not to hug it after all. She
was shy, her father and mother smelled so new. But then her

mother said they had a surprise for her. "Up in the guest room."
And she took Caitlin by the hand and led her back up the stairs
again. Caitlin had thought the surprise might be a new dress.
She'd pictured a red dress, little white buttons going all the way
down the front of it like tiny white china mushrooms, but when
she came into the guest room with her mother there was only a
baby in a basket. She had walked all around it, feeling more cross
than curious. And then, according to her mother—she herself
doesn't remember this at all, it was too long ago—she had said
to her mother, "Will it *bite?*"

But now her father and Faith were at the front door and calling her to come into the house so she could say goodbye to her
father. The sunlight flashed off Faith's glasses as she smiled down
at her, and when they went into the cool kitchen that smelled
the way she remembered (of olives and grey paint), Faith poured
her a glass of cold city milk and gave her a gingersnap. Then her
father kissed Faith goodbye and asked Caitlin to walk with him
out to the car.

But once her father had opened the car door, Caitlin stood
with her head bowed, the fingers of both hands hooked into the
left pocket of his jacket, and as she rhythmically rocked back and
forth in her new sneakers she kept pulling with her fingers on her
father's pocket as if her shy goal was to pull his pocket right off his
jacket. The sun was hot on her head, hot on the car hood, hot on
the black sticky tar at the edge of the new surface of the perfect
black road that ran past Faith and Kingsley's house with its tiny
diamond-paned windows that looked too much like the windows
in a storybook house where something sad had happened.

"What do you want to tell me?" Caitlin's father asked her,
and he half knelt beside her. But she couldn't speak and she
couldn't look up. "Caitie," he said, "you'll have to tell me. The

traffic's going to get bad and I'm going to have to leave right away."

And so she'd had no choice, and although it made her throat kill her she'd had to tell him that she didn't want to stay with Faith and Kingsley, she wanted to go home. It made her feel like such a baby, but it was the only way. And so he took her home.

How her mother reacted when she saw one big head and one little head in their old car as it swung into the laneway she doesn't recall, her memory of the incident simply stops with her father agreeing to take her back home.

Little Father and Mother

"And then one time," she says to Dulude, "when my parents were away for the evening in Saint John, and just before they were expected to come home, I talked Kevin into climbing into their bed with me so we could fall asleep there." She hadn't been thinking of sex games, and in fact nothing like that had happened, she had only been thinking of how surprised her father and mother would be when they walked into their bedroom and saw another father and mother asleep under their blankets. But what had possessed her, to do such a thing? Maybe she'd been thinking of Goldilocks. Who's been sleeping in my bed. Or maybe she'd thought her father and mother would wonder if they could be the real parents after all, when there were already two little parents sound asleep in their bed.

But they didn't get the joke, they were startled, and then, urging their sleepy children to their own narrow beds, frighteningly formal and correct with them. And Caitlin wasn't punished or lectured either; instead, she entered a period of being closely observed by her mother. By her mother! Who, it sometimes seemed to her, had never really looked at her before. But now her mother couldn't seem to stop watching her and was always wanting to know where are you going, where have you been, who were you with, you have to keep me informed of these things.

For the first time today, Dulude seems truly fascinated. "How old were you when this happened? This bed business?"

She isn't certain. "Maybe ten, maybe twelve, maybe eleven. . . ." Really, she has no idea at all. She could have been any age between nine and thirteen, but thirteen is definitely too old a number to mention. No, no, she couldn't have been thirteen, she was probably eleven. "I think I was ten."

"We must talk about this again the next session," Dulude tells her.

She sits up and blindly creeps her bare feet into her sandals. Then with her left hand she pulls her short slick hair back into a ducktail and then sits for a moment with her tiny slippery tail of hair pleasurably gripped in her fist. Once upon a time, years ago, she was a Goldilocks herself, her hair was that heavy and golden, and she wore it in a long heavy braid hanging all the way down to her tightly cinched waist. She wouldn't want to have long hair like that now though, she too much likes the way she's wearing it this summer, chopped off very short and ending in a damp little comma she can squeeze in the bottom end of her fist.

But she needs to ask Dulude something. She needs to ask him if it's true that Freud said that women who are whores in childhood turn into nuns in adulthood. She's planned to ask him this question at least twenty times, but no matter how often she rehearses it she can never quite find the courage to actually bring the damning words casually forth. Instead she says, "All that sex business I told you about a long time ago, you know what I mean, what happened in the woods with my brother and me—"

"Yes?" says Dulude, and he sounds a bit irritable, as if he is able to pick up the scent of a second-choice revelation and if that's all it's going to be, will she please get to the point quickly.

"I've always been under the impression that everything we did was all my idea, really, and that Kevin, even though he was the one who was older, was just sort of following along. . . ."

Dulude smiles as if to say, *Oh come now.* "It takes two to tango," he says, and he looks at his watch. "I'm sure it was at *least* as much your brother's idea as it was yours."

On the way out of his building, as she's passing by the ground-floor Xerox office that smells of the usual city-and-country mix, ether and woodshed—why do Xerox places always smell like this?—Caitlin remembers lying strapped to a stretcher while Kevin was lying strapped to a matching stretcher beside her. In the Saint John General Hospital this was, the year they were seven and eight. And then when it was almost time for them to be rolled into the operating room to get their tonsils pulled out, a freckled nurse with her hands poked into the hip pockets of her uniform came into the stretcher room to say hi to them. She hoisted herself up on one of the empty stretchers and sat with her white-stockinged legs hanging down and asked them silly riddles.

But then a cross older nurse with a white mask tied over her nose rushed in to wheel them away. "Who's going to go first?" she yelled at them, and Caitlin (terrified) pointed at Kevin and said, "He is."

Kevin's betrayed-looking eyes had stayed with her until it was her own turn to be wheeled down the frightening shining green hallway. She was positive that the look in his eyes meant he would die. And then she would die too, because she was a bad girl who had tricked him. In a big room with bright lights a man in a green smock put something that looked like a baseball cap without a sunshade on it over her nose and said this will just be for a minute, this is just a wee bit of ether, and then she thought she could hear him pouring a bottle of wine right down into the cap and then it wasn't like having a cap over her face after all, it was more like being in an igloo, an igloo made out of canvas with the strange dim light of bright sunlight coming through the snow or maybe she was at camp and was in a tent and he was saying this is going to make you feel really really swell, you'll see I'm not just whistling . . . and then she thought he was saying Dick, see, and she thought maybe the other doctor's name was Dick, or maybe the man in the smock was even reading from her school reader where it said Dick, see. . . . Spot run, and after the operation someone must have given her some grape juice to drink because she threw it all up into a silver basin and it didn't look like vomit at all, it looked exactly like grape juice. It smelled very bad, though, of bile and ether, and Kevin was in the next bed, also throwing up, and she couldn't talk because her throat hurt her too much, and then just before supper a man came to take Kevin's pee away in a tall silver jug.

THE BIG THREE

One night Caitlin's husband says to her, "What do you two talk about, anyway? You and Dulude?"

And she says, "Not what, honey, but *who*."

"Who then? Or should I say whom?"

And she longs to say to him, "Yoom. We talk about yoom."

But what she says instead is, "Oh, you know."

"No, I don't. That's why I'm asking."

"We talk about the Big Three. You and my mother and me. . . ."

SKIN

At school, Caitlin fell in love with a boy who wore a black suit jacket, too short in the sleeves. A tall boy who always looked sadly noble and alone. She imagined many scenes with him, scenes in which she was his girl and they were appearing in public together, holding hands. In her daydreams they didn't speak when they were alone, they didn't need to, they understood one another completely, without speech. She didn't imagine sex with this boy, he seemed too naturally proud and fine for sex, she didn't think of sex all that much any more anyway, it was just childish to be thinking of sex all the time.

She had to bike into Saint John every morning for classes, following behind Kevin, and when they got to school they pretended not to know one another. When Caitlin's Grade Nine class had to parade out of French on Thursday mornings and pass by the joking Grade Tens who were waiting to go in, Caitlin, although she was dimly aware of the presence of Kevin among the shuffling and disdainful older students, never looked up to greet him.

But one night in October he asked her if she knew a guy in Grade Ten named Danny Pepperdene. "He said something about you today. When you were coming out of French."

She knew him to see. She knew he was huge and freckled and that his orange hair was cut in a very short brush cut and that he

had eyes that were a pale and incredible blue. But he was important at school, he played on the football team, and so it puzzled
her to hear that he'd been talking about her. She said sharply,
warningly, "It wasn't something mean, was it?"

He didn't want to say.

"Tell me."

"Okay, but don't get mad at me."

She promised not to.

"So you're passing right by us, right? And he says, 'See that
one there? With the long braid hanging down her back? I'd like
to jump right on her.'"

She stared at him. Then she said in a careful voice, "Did you
say anything to him?"

"I said, 'Like fuck you will, you dumb jerk, that's my sister.'"

That night as Caitlin lay in her bed on the highway side of
the house and listened to the cars and trucks roaring by on their
way home from the late movie at the drive-in, she stared up at
the crazed schools of little lights darting back and forth across her
ceiling while she replayed the conversation between Danny
Pepperdene and Kevin over and over in her head. It seemed to
her she could think of it for a whole lifetime and still not be finished with thinking of it. She couldn't even imagine getting to
the point where she would *not* think of it. And yet she didn't at
all know what she thought.

After this, too, the fates conspired to torment her. She would
start to walk down the school's main hallway at four-thirty in the
afternoon and it would be deserted, but then at its far end a classroom door would open and a giant wearing giant loafers would
come walking toward her, his left hand holding his row of giant
books to his athletic left hip. He would look top-heavy and injured
in the ankles, the way boys on the football team always looked.

But the incredible blue eyes would look right through her, she wouldn't exist, or so she would imagine, because she wouldn't be looking at him at all by now, she'd instead be pretending to importantly search for something among the papers she was carrying held to her breasts. And for hours afterwards she would be shaken. She would write about it in her diary even, when she got home, give it the necessary significance, get down every detail of it.

She didn't forget about the noble lonely boy, she just didn't think she was really worthy any more, to adore him.

But then Danny Pepperdene got a girlfriend named Rita Petruccelli, an Italian girl who always wore the same pale-blue angora sweater and the same gored grey flannel skirt. Caitlin saw Danny Pepperdene waiting for Rita at her locker while in the most methodical, lazy, popular-girl way Rita stood at the long row of metal doors and combed down her black hair. And as she was combing, she was also looking unbelievably calm and sour and sure of herself, as if she knew the answer to everything, as if she'd figured the whole world out years ago and was not all that thrilled by it.

She had other boyfriends too. Danny, according to Kevin, was heartbroken by this and spent hours with her on weekend afternoons, lying with her in his arms on the couch in his parents' rec room, trying to talk her into not giving away so much skin.

"Skin?"

Kevin said it meant sex. Sex if a girl did it. She gave away skin.

Caitlin pictured Rita Petruccelli as a bolt of shining sand-coloured fabric, a sort of shantung, and a saleslady unrolling her and cutting out little square bits of shantung-skin and men buying them.

"He wants all the skin to just be for him."

VISITORS

The bad things that Caitlin was always afraid of at Christmas hadn't happened. What she feared most was always a fight between her father and mother. The other thing she feared was that some member of her family would say some too intimate thing to her, something that would expose her to some awful private revelation she would have no desire to hear—that her mother would tell her some awful thing about her father. Or that her father, by a certain kind of eyes-lowered silence, would sighingly imply some condemning thing about her mother. Or that Kevin would tell her some secret and really private and repulsive thing about himself. And she didn't want to hear any of it. She really did not want to know private things about the people in her family, she just wanted them to be a normal family and do the things that people in normal families did.

Everything her mother did enraged her, though, and she kept finding herself wanting to rephrase, inside in her own head, things her mother had said, rephrase them in a voice mocking her mother's voice: high-pitched and nervous. One afternoon back in the fall, just before the first snowfall had put an end to the biking into Saint John to go to school, she had dipped down from her bike as she was riding down the lane from the highway because she had caught sight of her mother standing up on the hill beside the old barn, hugging herself in the cold breeze and talking to a big man in jeans and a yellow turtleneck. But just after she'd crossed the plank bridge over the brook, Caitlin had figured out who the man was. It was Horse McCrae. Her mother had waved and called to her to come up the hill and say hello to him.

But Caitlin had instead veered off the lane and walked her bike through the field of tall grasses down by the river, pretending not to hear, staring straight ahead and yanking the bike along roughly because its spokes kept getting snarled up with the dead grass in the low swampy part of the field. It was hard to look aloof while trying to snap the bike free of the tough grasses and so she'd decided to drop it in the shed that was halfway to the beach instead of bringing it up the hill and parking it in the porch at the side of the house. Then for good measure she'd walked along the beach to Puddingtons' store for a Coke.

And the amazing thing was that her mother, who was always such an absolute stickler for good behaviour, hadn't reproached her at suppertime. Hadn't said, "Now why in heaven's name didn't you come up the hill and say hello to Bill McCrae? I just can't understand how you could be so incredibly impolite." Caitlin mimicked her mother's voice inside her own head. How can you have been so disgustingly rude, the voice said. To poor *Horse*.

Two nights after Christmas, company was invited for supper, friends of Caitlin's parents who were trying to talk them into moving their antique business to the town of Arnprior, Ontario. They had a tall bashful son with wildly polite eyes and a permanently blushing skin. He was a student at Rothesay Collegiate School for Boys and he wore a navy blazer and grey flannels and he was hard to be around because he was so painfully correct. Whenever Caitlin came into the den he would get to his feet and then he wouldn't seem to know at what point he should permit himself to be seated again. It made Caitlin decide not to go in there any more. But then her mother called her to come in and pass around the almonds and walnuts. Caitlin, in a long-waisted navy blue taffeta dress that was too big for her, tried to repress her nervous resentment as she obeyed her.

Becca was in there too, lying on the floor and colouring a

picture she had drawn of some piggy people lying on their backs on a pink beach by the ocean.

The boy's father seemed to be really crazy about Becca's piggy people. He said, "It's plain to see this little lady has a whole lot of talent." And the boy's mother, who was wearing a rakishly tilted green tam and a frilly green blouse almost the same lime colour as Becca's ocean, said, "And she's going to grow up to be quite the little heartbreaker too."

Caitlin was to be allowed to make the whole dinner by herself, and had planned meat loaf. "Just something simple," her mother had said. "After all the feasting." But the fact that a boy her own age was going to be eating it was making her feel sick with dread. She was convinced that this boy (whose name was Derek) would be the kind of boy her mother would want her to marry. Someone polite, someone who attended a private school for boys.

She tried to imagine being married to him, she pictured herself tying on a quilted pink dressing gown and coming into a sunny kitchen to make Derek his breakfast on a cold and clear Monday morning in the future. But he was already sitting at the breakfast table, already in his blazer and grey flannels, reading the morning paper.

When she came into the room he stood. She got out the frying pan and the eggs and the butter and started to make an omelet while Derek stayed standing. She didn't know how to tell him to sit down. She imagined herself saying, "You may be seated now." Or perhaps she would merely say, "You don't really need to do that."

It was the same thing at bedtime. When she came into their bedroom in her long satin nightgown, Derek (still in his blazer and flannels) again stood. It was embarrassing. Or it could be.

She wouldn't know how to ask him if he was planning on coming to bed.

She opened the refrigerator to check on the bowl of heaped meat and saw that it was hazy with a red fog from the raw reddish pink of the beef. She had already sliced the onions and mushrooms to be added to it before she slipped it into the oven and wondered if she should mix them in right now or wait a bit longer. The mushrooms looked like little white paper cutouts of themselves and were layered all around the onion rings on a dinner plate that sat next to the pie-dough. She didn't want to be in the den with Derek, but all the same she felt a bit weird just sitting all by herself out here in the kitchen. Like a cook or a maid or something. So that when Kevin came in to fetch a second bottle of sherry she took this as her signal to start scrubbing the potatoes.

He said in a low voice, "What do you think of Derek?"

"I don't know," she whispered back. "He's so polite he makes me feel sort of nervous."

"I know, the poor guy's such a drip you kind of feel like you ought to take pity on him."

He lifted a bottle of sherry down from the wine cupboard and tucked it under an arm. He was wearing the red necktie their parents had given him for Christmas, and looked like a boy she barely knew.

"Do you think that's true? What Derek's mother said about Becca?"

"What? That she has a whole lot of talent? Hell no. I mean, she's only a little kid, so how can anyone even tell yet?"

"No, no, not that, the other thing, the thing that Derek's *mother* said, that Becca is going to grow up to be quite the little heartbreaker."

He didn't even have to stop to think about it. "Sure," he said. "Come on, you have to admit it, she's the cute type." And he started to take off with the sherry.

"Kev?" But she could see by his eyes that all he wanted was to be with the life and laughter back in the den and so the smart thing to do would be to invent some quick little thing that she needed him to do for her. Unscrew a lid on a bottle of pickles, say, or lift the heaviest casserole dish down from the cupboard. But she decided to say what she'd planned to say in the first place: "What type am I?"

In spite of his hurry, he stopped in the doorway to study her. She could see him weighing her face and his words in his eyes.

"You're more the plain type," he said.

And then he was gone.

She felt slowed down by an awful heaviness after he went back to the den, and for a while she didn't do anything, she only sat at the kitchen table on the chair closest to the window that looked out on the snowed-in back garden. There was a little tam of snow sitting on the top of each of the three propane gas tanks that stood in a short row against the garden's west wall. She knew the type she was, the type older people, especially older men, seemed to like. Last summer a painter had visited the antique store and she'd helped him choose milk-glass vases as presents for friends of his back in Toronto, and that night after supper her mother had told her that the painter had said, "What a beautiful daughter you have"—sounding, thought Caitlin, like the wolf in "Red Riding Hood," and so she could all too easily imagine him saying, "What a beautiful *big* daughter you have, my dear. . . ." He'd also said that the next time he came back to these parts he would like to paint her. But the painter was old, maybe even in his forties, and the thought of how stiff and self-conscious she'd be if she had to pose for him made her feel as if she could barely breathe. Maybe he would expect her to pose without any clothes on. She was afraid she would be too reserved to tell him that she really wouldn't want to do that kind of thing.

But at this point she remembered the supper and realized she'd left things much too late and now she didn't even have time to preheat the stove for the potatoes and so she tossed them like bowling balls into the cold oven and turned on the gas. Then the meat loaf: she turned the plate of mushrooms and onion slices upside-down over the meat bowl, then kneaded everything in with her hands, scooped the meat mixture into a pan, walked the heel of her right hand all over it, pressing the meat loaf hard into all the corners, then shoved the pan into the oven with the potatoes. Then started to slice the apples for the pie.

But then she had trouble finding the cinnamon and nutmeg, and was nearly tearful with worry that she would not find them. The last thing in the world she wanted to do was go into the den and ask her mother where they were. She dragged a kitchen chair over to the cabinets and climbed up on it so she could poke far back into the cupboard where the spices were kept.

The kitchen was too small. To make things easier, and to save on cupboard space, her father had nailed six rows of nails from the beams in the ceiling so that each mug and cup could be hung from its own personal nail. Caitlin's anxious shoulder, as she backed up from ransacking the spice cupboard, hit one of the teacups and it smashed on the floor. *Damn!* Did anyone hear it? The Glasgow Orpheus Choir was singing in its massed majestic way, shouting out some carol about masters in these halls, here we sing today, today. If Becca is a little heartbreaker, then what am I? She thought her father would say she was a little dish-breaker. She jumped down to the floor and gathered up the shards of broken cup and scooped them into a paper bag and dumped them into the garbage pail. But then she decided she'd better check on the potatoes and she pulled open the oven door. Damn, damn, damn, *damn,* the damn oven was still cold. She couldn't believe so much bad luck could happen to one person in one afternoon. She grabbed a match from the little pottery jug beside the stove and struck it with such fury against the jug's unglazed bottom that it leapt into flame on the first try. Then she dropped into a deep curtsy to the oven to light it.

A great boom was heard by all the laughing guests out in the den, and when they heard it, they all jumped up and ran toward the explosion.

Caitlin was standing in the middle of the tiny kitchen, her eyebrows and eyelashes almost completely singed off and every cup teetering on the head of every nail, swinging horribly, delicately, trying to decide whether to hang or fall.

DULUDE AGAIN

It's spring again and Dulude's voice speaks to Caitlin from behind her couch: "A really quite intriguing fantasy—the one about the young man who was more or less constantly erect."

Does he mean her brother? "Who?" she asks him.

"The polite young man."

"Which polite young man?"

"The polite young man who came to dinner."

"But I didn't see him as being sexual at *all.*"

"Your unconscious clearly has other ideas on the matter."

Oh please, she wants to say to him. Why must we always be so utterly simple-minded?

But it's in Dulude's nature to persist: "In childhood you saw him as sexual."

"Oh, in childhood," she says. As if to say: "Oh *that*."

But there are also times when she does in fact feel grateful to Dulude for his stubborn simplicity. Sometimes it leads somewhere. Of course there are also days when it's deeply boring to be here. Boring on some days, euphoric on others. There's also a question she could never ask Dulude: How can so much euphoria and so much boredom exist side by side? As for the euphoria, it always seems to come from discovering that the events of her past that felt most unbearable while they were happening to her have turned into the very events that now make her feel the most tenderness for her younger self. Many of these memories are fixed in adolescence (*Surprise! Surprise!* cries her older self), and one of them—one of the most shameful ones (and therefore one of her favourites)—goes back to the late fall of the year she was in Grade Ten, not long after she and Kev had moved back into town to stay with Faith and Kingsley over the winter. Kev was billeted in a big room on the top floor of the house—to get to it he had to climb up a nearly vertical ship's ladder—and Caitlin (now that Gloria was away at Horton Academy) was put into Gloria's old room. But there was another resident in the house over the winters as well—a cousin of Faith's named Pat—a bedridden and pretty grey-haired woman who owned a whole family of scalloped pink satin bed jackets and whose face always wore a cultivated but menstrual look.

In her suitcase Caitlin had also packed pink things, a pink slip and a pink sweater and a pink taffeta shift of her mother's, made over for her to wear to school parties. But she hated it, hated the way it carried the scent of her mother in it, hated the way it carried the damning taint of having been altered. It made her look like an idiot. An idiot from the country. It had had sleeves added to it, pink taffeta stovepipes, when she looked at herself in the mirror in it she looked as if she didn't know how to bend her arms in the stovepipes, the first thing she did when she got into town was hang it in the darkened end of the closet.

BLACK SATIN WILLOW

Gloria wrote Caitlin a letter. Its opening words were "From Mother I understand that you are not particularly happy." Caitlin carried it around in her coat pocket for days. It seemed to be a kind letter, but she was bewildered by it and each time she read it she would feel, all over again, that her feelings had been hurt. As for happiness, it still seemed to her to be a faraway thing, safely lying in wait for her in adulthood. When I'm nineteen, twenty, she thought, then I'll be happy, have beautiful clothes, boyfriends, but for now she only felt ashamed, she couldn't bear to think that Faith had been secretly watching her and writing Gloria a letter about her, having come to the conclusion that she was not happy.

And in fact now that she knew she was being kept under observation, she began to do something she realized she'd been wanting to do all along, she began to spend at least an hour in the bathroom every afternoon after school, experimenting with make-up. And in the evenings she would go to Gloria's closet and peek in at her row of hung dresses, at the way they bloomed exploded pink and blue in their zippered long clear storage boxes. There were costumes from plays Gloria had been in, too (at Horton Academy she belonged to Drama Club) and one night when Faith and Kingsley were out at a concert, Caitlin undid her school skirt and blouse to step into the dress she loved best, the one that made her think of a strapless black satin willow. She held her breath as she pulled up its zipper, and when she went over to the mirror in it she felt tender, in love with her own body. She leaned toward her breasts, hugged them into plumpness. Then turned, turned again, picked up a pencil and poked it into her mouth, sucked on it deeply. Then removed it, exhaled, held it out at an angle while she drooped her eyes at herself in Gloria's mirror. Her mouth tasted of eraser and of the thin band of tin separating the eraser from pencil wood. And so she only kept holding out the pencil and now and then exhaling while trying out different poses. But after nine or ten minutes spent parading and preening, she began to feel breathless, too tightly encased. Gloria was petite, more petite than she was, she had to admit it, and Gloria's dress was really much much too tight, so tight that she was beginning to feel totally suffocated in it, and now, like a punishment for trying to take possession of what didn't belong to her, the zipper all at once wouldn't budge, and so she had to back up to Gloria's dressing table and hitch herself painfully up onto its glass top and then, gasping slightly, walk her hips backwards until she was almost flush with her own back in Gloria's mirror. Peering over a shoulder she winged back her elbows and took whimpering little yanks at the zipper's metal tag until her arms ached unbearably. But she wasn't able to jiggle it. And so she did a cautiously wobbly slither off the dresser and then went over to her closet to draw out her dressing gown and tie it weakly on.

Then she stepped out into the hallway.

She didn't glance over toward Pat's room, but she knew that Pat's open door gave her a clear view of everything that went on out in the hall. She could only hope and pray that Pat would think the strip of black undulating beneath the dressing gown was a black nightgown.

And then in a voice that she tried to keep from sounding high and trembly, she called up to Kevin, "Kev! Can you come down here for a minute?"

"What for?"

"I need help with an algebra equation!"

He called down that she should bring it up to *him* then, he was not her servant.

But she knew that she couldn't possibly climb such a steep ladder in the slick narrow dress. "I can't! And I have to ask you something about history too!"

He would come down then. But he was busy right now. "Be down in twenty minutes."

She went back into her room. What time had Faith and Kingsley left for the concert? At least two hours ago, maybe even three. And Pat had been gawking at her too, she was sure of it, she was sure she suspected something. She closed her door with a guilty stealth she hoped would be mistaken for tact, then sat and prayed that Kevin could get her out of the dress before Faith and Kingsley came back. But what if he couldn't? What if she had to lie in it the whole night, sleepless and breathless? And then go down to breakfast with her yellow school sweater pulled over the top of it and the black satin skirt bunched into her underpants and one of her fat plaid school skirts buttoned on over it?

But at long last she heard the hitch and squeak of Kevin's descent down the ladder.

She opened her door just enough for him to squeeze his way in, then quickly closed it again. When she undid the ties of her dressing gown he gaped at the gleam of the black dress beneath it.

"I can't get out of it," she whispered. "You'll have to help me."

He whispered back hoarsely, "So why did you put it on in the first place then? It's not even yours!"

She wanted to scream at him, wanted to moan *shut up, shut up, shut up, shut up,* but she couldn't, she was depending on him, and so she only said in a commanding low whisper, "Hurry!"

She could feel him at her back, jiggling and pulling at the zipper with fierce little yanks. It was both consoling and terrifying to know that he was as desperate as she was. They both understood social shame. They both understood that they were the representatives of their own family while living in the house of another family. He whispered, "I can't budge it."

"Your knife!"

"But won't that wreck it?"

She closed her eyes. But then she said, "No, do it."

She heard him snap up the blade at the same moment that they could both hear the sound they'd been dreading—the confident swing of car into gravel—and so in unison they began to urgently whimper, no time to lose, Kevin cursing and Caitlin whispering, "Oh God, God, God, please God, please oh please *hurry, hurry,*" which made Kevin hiss back: "Shut up, shut up, shut up, shut *up,*" but she began to breathe again as she felt the blade track a seam, and by the time Faith and Kingsley had come into the house and had finished doing all the little end-of-day things—yawning, locking up, running themselves quick bedtime drinks of cold water— Kevin had hitched himself up to his loft again and Caitlin had rolled the slippery black dress into a white bath towel and stuffed it behind the flounced skirt of her bed and was brushing her hair as she stood at her window, pretending to be calm and wearing nothing but a real nightgown under her dressing gown.

The following weekend she carried the butchered dress home

in her knapsack. But it couldn't be mended, the cut had been made in the black satin skin of it, not down the seam. Her mother said, "Please don't make us feel we have to be ashamed of you, not after all the great kindness Faith and Kingsley have shown to the people in this family," and she understood then that nothing (or next to nothing) was being paid to Faith and Kingsley for Kevin's and her room and board, it was why her mother was always telling her to be sure she helped with the dishes every night and to always be polite and remember to thank Faith and Kingsley for everything. And then both her parents told her she would have to make a confession to Faith and that if she hadn't told her the truth by the following Friday when her father would be coming to pick her up for the weekend, her father would have no choice but to tell her himself.

NIGHT AND CONFESSION

Every night she planned to confess, every night she faked cutting her toenails till well after midnight.

On Thursday night Faith came to her door: "Darling, time to turn out your light." Stripped down to her slim navy slip, she stood in Caitlin's doorway. Her eyebrows were looking more demanding than usual, she'd been creaming her face. Then she came into Caitlin's room, sat sidesaddle on the end of her bed. She was pretty, even if she was quite old and had to wear thick rimless glasses. She wore pretty clothes. Tonight she was also wearing high-heeled backless slippers made out of a stylish navy leather. She even had perfect legs, although Caitlin had never actually noticed them until she'd overheard her father say to someone once, at a Christmas party, "Faith has the world's most fabulous legs." Now she watched Faith cross one fabulous leg over the other and take off her glasses because she'd got a dab of cream on one of the lenses. Then heard her voice say, "Darling, you've been staying up past midnight every night the whole week. Is something the matter?"

Caitlin looked down at her hands in her lap and her tears gave her double the number of fingers. She knew she had reached the point where she now had no choice: no matter how much she longed to let the opportunity pass, this was the right moment to tell Faith what a fool she had been. But at the end of her confession, Faith only gave her a brief sideways hug and said, "Oh, darling—Gloria doesn't even care about that silly old black dress any more!"

Caitlin had to turn sharply away from Faith then, she was so stunned by the smile she could hear in her voice as she tried to console her. Being too young to know that her smile was only an announcement of how much she'd feared worse: pregnancy, rape, a child's body ripped open.